Dad, Can You Hear Me Now? It's Pal

Back Cover: Author Photograph
Courtesy Hansen Fine Portraits
Orange City, Florida

Front Cover: Photograph by the Author
Order this book online at www.trafford.com
or email orders@trafford.com

Most Trafford titles are also available at major online book retailers.

Printed in Victoria, BC, Canada.

ISBN: 978-1-4269-2252-7 (sc)

ISBN: 978-1-4269-2253-4 (dj)

Library of Congress Control Number: 2009912627

*Our mission is to efficiently provide the world's finest, most comprehensive book publishing
service, enabling every author to experience success. To find out how to publish your book, your
way, and have it available worldwide, visit us online at www.trafford.com*

Trafford rev. 11/19/2009

 www.trafford.com

North America & international
toll-free: 1 888 232 4444 (USA & Canada)
phone: 250 383 6864 ♦ fax: 812 355 4082

To my late wife Gladys,
Our children Dennis, Cheryl, and Gary
And especially to our dog Pal

Contents

INTRODUCTION

A Message From Pal

It is interesting to listen to the owners of pets talk to us dogs. Some people choose to scream, others to quietly beg. The purpose, I suppose, is to get our attention to do a task that satisfies the nice, and the not so nice, pet owners.

Take me for example; my name is Pal. I've been living the good life since shortly after my birth with a kind and very loving couple. His name is Lee; I call him my Dad. Gladys is his wife; I call my Mom. Yes, I know they are not my Mom and Dad, but what else would I call them?

Usually they refer to me as their cute little puppy. Actually, I have been living a very good dog's life with this couple for almost my entire life. They purchased me when I was a brand new baby pup. *"Golly, I love these two so much!"*

Dad has attempted to teach me what a dog's life is all about. How he knows that, I have no idea. Perhaps he has read it in the book he purchased about my breed. For the most part his teaching has succeeded, but only because I agree with his sometimes strange teaching ideas. The real reason I agree to do anything is my Dad gives me good treats to eat. Most pets will do anything their owner's desire, provided they are given a reward. Otherwise, *forget it!*

Many movies and television stories have talking animals as their main characters. I know this is true because Mom and I watch movies on television all the time. I'm certainly not a movie star, but I can talk too. *So there*! Mom talks to me all the time and I talk to her, but she can't hear me. That's a real bummer. Did you know all animals and birds talk among themselves? You would not believe some of the stories I hear from my fellow critters. Why, once I even listened to the problems of a big snake that was in our backyard. But, I am digressing a bit.

It took some doing for me to get Dad to write this story. I would have done it myself except, if you haven't noticed, we dogs have no fingers. Besides, Dad doesn't allow me to touch his precious laptop computer!

The situations that follow are some of *my* most memorable experiences. Oh, sure, there have been other things happen in my home over the last six years, but for the most part, they are just ordinary daily happenings. Enjoy my story as I talk about our happy times, and yes, a few sad ones as well.

CHAPTER 1

. . . .

What to Do Next?

Once upon a time, in the land of Deland, Florida, there lived a very lonely lady: Mary Douglas, with her daughter Ginger.

"Wait just a minute." Dad said. "You can't begin the book like this. It's not a fairytale book; it's your true story."

"Okay, how's this Dad, for a storybook beginning?"

In the small Florida town of Deland, ***once upon a time***, there lived a very lonely lady: Mary Douglas, with her daughter Ginger.

"No, no, no! Stop with the *once upon a time* thing!"

"Okay, Dad, how's this?" In the small Florida town of Deland, there lived a very lonely lady, Mary Douglas. She had a daughter named Ginger.

"That's much better. Now you may continue with the story."

Mary had to find a way to earn extra money quickly. Her husband had passed away recently and left Mary with only a small amount of savings and a very small insurance income. Unfortunately that would not fill the gap of all her monthly housing expenses. Mary wondered how she was going to survive on such a limited insurance income.

Mary, a petite lady in her forties, and her teenage daughter Ginger, sat in the kitchen in their small house, eating breakfast while discussing the issue. For just a moment Mary considered selling the house. But because the house was nearly paid off, she felt that would not be the smartest move. Besides, she said to Ginger, "You wouldn't be happy living in an apartment or a smaller house, would you?"

Quick to reply, Ginger said. "I could never leave this house, Mom; it has too many memories of Dad. Please don't ever think of selling our house."

"Well, Ginger, we have to come up with some way to earn a little extra money each month. Have you any suggestions?"

Ginger thought and thought about the question her mother was asking.

"We could raise birds, Mom." Ginger suggested. "Talking parakeets or singing canaries would be a good way to earn extra money."

"No," her mother said. "They are much too noisy and make such a mess in the house."

"Well then, how about raising rabbits or guinea pigs?"

"No, Ginger, there's not enough money when you sell them. Besides, they smell awful."

Ginger thought and thought and finally exclaimed, "Mommy, I have always wanted a little doggie, but Daddy said no, *never!* Now, Mommy, we could get a small lady dog and she could have puppies that we could sell."

"*Uh-huh.*" Mary thought to herself. "Ginger, you know, I always wanted a little dog myself, but you are right: your Daddy always said no. If we buy a lady dog, Ginger, would you help me take care of her?"

Ginger exclaimed, "Oh, yes, Mommy, I will, I will. Thank you, thank you so much."

For the next few days Mary and Ginger went all over the countryside looking for the perfect small lady dog. All they looked at were either too big or too tiny, and much too expensive. Upon arriving home late in the day Mary saw there was a message light blinking on her telephone answering machine. It was a message from a man who had heard she was looking for a lady dog. He explained he had to move and could not take Lady with him. Lady was his dog's name. If she wanted his dog, she could have her if Mary would promise to give her a good home *forever*.

Mary wrote down the man's name and address, and the very next day an excited Mary and Ginger drove to the address.

"Good morning." Franklin Morrow said. He was an older dark skinned man with long, totally white hair, who Mary assumed to be in his late seventies. "You must be the ladies that have come to take my Lady to her new home."

Lady immediately ran up to greet Mary and Ginger, wagging her tail and wanting the attention of the visitors.

Mary was the first to notice. "Mr. Morrow, she is so beautiful and friendly — and just the size we wanted: She's not too big and not too tiny. Her color is just lovely." With that, Mary stroked Lady's soft dark brown hair and her cream colored chest, pulling slightly on her long tail. "Just beautiful, but she looks like she is going to have puppies pretty soon."

"That she is." Said Mr. Morrow with a trembling voice, while fighting to hold back tears. "That's one of the reasons I must find her a home quickly. The old folk's home where I'm going won't allow dogs, definitely not a dog that is going to have a litter of puppies."

Mary said. "Mr. Morrow, on the telephone I didn't ask you what breed of dog she was."

Mr. Morrow paused for a moment before saying, "Mary, one reason I am giving her to you is you never asked how much money I wanted, and you didn't ask what kind of dog she was. You accepted her for who she is and that made me happy. She is a pure bred, registered Shih Tzu. And yes, I did say, I was giving her to you free"

"What kind?" Ginger asked brushing a loose strand of her long blonde hair back off her face.

"A Shih Tzu, Ginger, and it is pronounced *Sheed-zoo*. These dogs go way back to the seventeenth century in China. The name means '*Lion Dog.*' It's not because they hunted lions, but because their face, with a full grown facial beard, resembles a lion. They were the favorite house dog of royal families during the Manchu Dynasty. Eventually they made it to England and then to America."

"Wow, Mom," Ginger exclaimed, "we had a history lesson *and* a beautiful dog. Thank you so much, Mr. Morrow. We will take *very* good care of Lady! I promise!"

Mary relayed her financial dilemma story to Mr. Morrow who understood all too well the problem. He had experienced a similar situation after his wife died several years ago.

For a bit she exchanged her thoughts about the life Lady

would have in her new home. It didn't take long for the old gentleman to realize that Mary and Ginger would be the perfect new owners of Lady. Without reluctance Mr. Morrow gave Mary Lady's food and drink dish, a bag of dog food, and a few of her play toys.

Mary and Ginger hugged and thanked Mr. Morrow as Lady jumped willingly into Mary's car. It was a sad day for Mr. Morrow, but a happy day for Mary and Ginger.

It was April 9, 2003; when Lady began the process of having her pups.

Ginger awoke early Saturday morning. In her pajamas and just barely awake, she was yawning and wiping the sleep from her eyes as she slowly walked toward the kitchen. Running her hands through her long blond, not yet combed hair, she went to the refrigerator to begin preparing her usual breakfast of cereal and milk. The sun had not provided enough daylight for her to see clearly in the kitchen, so she reached for the light switch.

With the room now fully lighted, Ginger noticed Lady lying fully stretched out on her side. "Good morning, Lady. Did you have a good night's sleep?" Ginger said. There was not even a slight response from Lady — Not even a glance acknowledging her presence. "That's odd, Lady, aren't you feeling well?" As she was saying that, Ginger stepped over the small kitchen gate that kept Lady from venturing into the rest of the house.

As Ginger reached down to touch Lady, Lady raised her head slowly while making a quiet moaning sound. *"Mom, ... Mom,* come quick!" exclaimed a very excited Ginger. "I think Lady is trying to deliver her pups."

Mary, dressed in her nightgown, raced quickly to the kitchen to see for herself. "You are so right, Ginger. Come, we should go into the living room away from her. She should be quite capable of delivering her pups on her own. We need to give her some privacy. I talked to the veterinarian last week, and he said if she has any delivery trouble, we will hear her crying. The veterinarian said he would come to the house if we needed help with the delivery."

About an hour went by before Mary heard the sound of Lady licking and cleaning her newborn children. "Come, Ginger; let's quietly see how Lady is doing."

Lady continued cleaning her three new babies. A brown and white male and two black and white girls were squirming around in the large box Mary had placed on the kitchen floor before going to bed. Mary had gone to a furniture store earlier in the week and picked up a big empty sofa box that would be big enough for Lady to sleep in. Ginger and Mary had cut the sides of the box down to just a few inches off the floor. Mary had several old large beach towels which she placed in the box making it a cozy nesting place for Lady. "That way," Mary reasoned, "Lady would be comfortable when it was time for the delivery of her babies." Lady was such a sensible girl. At this particular time Lady was making good use of the beach towels.

In the box, one of the pups was yelling, although no one could hear him, "Hello there, anybody home! ... *Hey there*, I can't see a thing! ... Hello, anybody! Somebody please talk to me!" The little brown and white newborn puppy cried. The new pup said, "One minute it's nice and warm and dark and the next minute I'm freezing in this big cardboard box.

What happened to make it so cold all of the sudden? Come on, *somebody* … I can hear you talking, so *talk* to me."

"Oh, Mom, aren't they just the cutest little balls of fur you ever did see?" exclaimed Ginger.

Mary was quick to see where Ginger's conversation was going and replied, "Yes, Ginger, they are very cute. You do know we can't keep the three of them *and* Lady. You do know that, don't you? Because I really do need the money we'll get when we sell them?"

Hanging her head down so as to not show the tears, Ginger cried, "Yes, mother, I know, but couldn't we just keep one?"

Mary, fully expecting this kind of scene. explained, "Ginger, in about six or seven weeks the baby pups will be old enough to be weaned from drinking Lady's milk. The three of them will begin eating puppy food and will require a lot of attention by a veterinarian. Ginger baby, we couldn't afford to do all the things these baby pups will need. Besides, this is what we decided to do to earn extra money."

Understanding, but still not liking the answer, Ginger reluctantly said, "Yes, Mom, we agreed. I'm sorry, Mommy."

Again from in the box a very impatient voice of the newborn pup called out, "Come on, somebody, get me a blanket! I'm freezing!"

The very quiet, but calming voice of Lady, his mother, said, "Little fellow, who do you think is going to hear you. You're a dog, not a person. We dogs can only talk to each other. Now settle down." Lady reached over to the brown and white whining fellow with her paw and began to pull the boy close. "Come on, little boy; snuggle close to my fur and I'll keep you warm."

He schooched under Lady's chin, between her front legs, and said, as though apologizing, "Now, that's much better. I can't see you yet, but I'm guessing you are much bigger than me. Right?"

Lady, somewhat irritated by his behavior said, "Little fellow, I'm your mother and you can call me Mom. And yes, I am much bigger than you. By tonight your eyes will begin to open and you will see a wonderful big world around you. I can see from the start you are going to be trouble. Now, when I talk to you or call you, I expect you to listen. Do you hear me?"

"Yes, Mom, I hear you." There was a long pause with nothing being said. Suddenly the little fellow whispered, "Hey, Mom, I'm hungry. Is there anything to eat around here?"

"Yes, my little bundle of trouble, I have milk. I think that's what I'll call you, *Trouble*. That name will suit you just fine." Lady began to move Trouble around and behind her front legs. That is the place all three of the pups could begin to suckle her milk.

As Trouble began the hunt for the milk spigot, a slightly frightened Trouble said, "Hey, Mom, I don't know how to tell you this, but there is some creepy, fuzzy thing here. *What is it, Mom?* Matter of fact, there is a bunch of fuzzy things here. *Help, Mom!*"

"Relax, Trouble; it is only your two sisters. They are the same as you, only they are girls. I had them the same time I had you. Now grab hold of one of those drinking things and suck hard; the milk will make you big and strong."

"*This is amazing!* My Mom has enough warm milk for all three of us."

With considerable effort, Trouble finally figured out how to get the faucet turned on.

After drinking until satisfied, all three puppies lay on the now freshly clean bath towels which were on the floor of the cardboard box. Apparently Trouble drank too fast because he suddenly let out a loud … "*Burp!*"

"Ah, that's better." he said. "Guess I'm supposed to say, 'Excuse me!' I must have had a big bubble in my belly."

Trouble found out his mom was right. The next day his eyes were open, and he could see people in the room, and he could see his sisters for the first time. In fact, he could see his sisters close up. The two female puppies were climbing all over Trouble. "Hey, Mom, two against one, that's not fair. *Mom*, tell them to stop."

"Now, Trouble, they are just playing. Behave yourself and be nice to them."

"Sure, Mom! Come on, girls, stop it! One of you got your foot in my ear. *Now cut it out!*"

The weeks went by, and the three of them were already beginning to grow bigger.

Mary and Ginger enjoyed sitting at the kitchen table, watching the baby pups play. "They are so cute, Mom; it's a shame we have to sell them."

"Yes, Ginger, I know, but we had an agreement. It's about time to think about selling them." Mary said. "I think I will put an ad in the newspaper, advertising them for $650 each."

"*That much?*" Ginger questioned.

"Remember, Lady is a pure bred female Shih Tzu, and I have the registration papers for each of them. That makes them worth much more. It also gives me a chance to negotiate the price down if I have to."

"Hey, Mom." said Trouble. "Did you hear what Mary just said?"

"Yes, Trouble, I did. That's what people do. We mother dogs give them puppies and they sell them for money. Mary needs money badly and she will sell the three of you."

With tears in his eyes Trouble said, "But, Mommy, I don't want to leave you, *ever!*"

"It will be okay, Trouble. I'm sure a very nice family will take you in." Lady reassured him.

Still not satisfied with his Mom's answer, he said, "*Will one family take my sisters and me?*"

"No, Trouble, that almost never happens." said Lady, hoping to end the conversation. "Besides, Trouble, more than one of you in one house would be double trouble for whoever takes you home. When you guys grow up, you would be fighting all the time … *then what … I'll* tell you what. One of you, or maybe all of you, would end up in the dog pound. You don't know what that is, but believe me, you don't want to go there. That's the end of the conversation, Trouble! Okay!"

"Okay, Mom, whatever you say."

CHAPTER 2

. . . .

A New Family for One

The telephone was ringing as Mary and Ginger came in the door. They had been to the grocery store where Mary had placed a sales flyer on the grocery store bulletin board, advertising the pups. Racing to the ringing telephone, an out of breath Mary said, "Hello … Oh, hi, Cheryl. Sorry I'm so out of breath … what can I do for you?" Cheryl was inquiring about Mary's puppies which were for sale.

Cheryl knew Mary from the various church activities they did together. Cheryl and her two brothers decided they would buy a small pup for their mother's birthday. Cheryl's Mom's birthday wasn't until May 29 so the timing was just right. The pups would be weaned from their mother by then. The pups were old enough now for possible buyers to visit and take a look at the new puppies.

The telephone conversation with Cheryl ended with

Mary saying, "Sure, Cheryl, next Friday would be great. … Your mom and dad may choose either one of the three, one boy or one of the two girls. See you late Friday afternoon. Bye now."

About two o'clock Friday afternoon, as promised, Cheryl and her Mom and Dad arrived in the driveway of Mary's house. Cheryl's Mom, Gladys, was anxious to see who her new best friend would be. The last dog Gladys had was a little chocolate brown poodle that lived with her in Pennsylvania and had come along when she moved to Florida. She knew just how attached a person can get to a pet. Earlier in Gladys' life she had a canary, and later in Florida, in addition to the poodle, she had a cockatoo. But now, many years later, she had no pets and she was looking forward to seeing what kind of dog her children had picked out for her.

After brief introductions all around, Mary and Ginger took the three visitors to see the new baby Shih Tzu's. Gladys didn't know how to pronounce the breed's name, so Ginger made it a point to help her say the kind of dog. Ginger, taught to respect her elders said, "Miss Gladys, they are called *Sheed-Zoo's*."

More confused than ever, Gladys said, "We'll just give the one we choose a real name and that's what I'll call it."

Gladys, Cheryl, and Cheryl's Dad, Lee, looked at the three puppies in amazement, not knowing how to choose one. Lee said, "If I was the one to choose, I'd choose the male. You have less medical problems with a male Shih Tzu."

Lee said that as though he knew something about the Shih Tzu breed, but actually he had never even heard of them before today. The truth is he was right; however, just ask any veterinarian. Females have a lot more problems than male dogs.

Gladys liked the brown and white one because he seemed to be the most active. Little did she know that Trouble is what his mother called the tiny little boy dog. Lee made the final decision for Gladys and said to Cheryl, "If that is the one your mother wants, that's it. He looks like a little snowball playing there in the box. I'd like to call him *Snowball*."

Trouble looked at his mother who was peacefully lying in the far corner of their box and said, using a rather harsh tone in his voice, "Snowball, what kind of sissy name is that —Snowball?"

His sisters looked at Trouble and poked fun at him, saying, "Oh, Snowball, your doggie friends are going to love that: 'Come here, you cute little Snowball!'

"Knock it off, you two! At least somebody wants me! Ha-ha!"

"No, I don't think Snowball is the right name for him." Gladys said, "He looks like my pal; I'll call him Pal. After all, I had a canary called Pal and a cockatoo called Pal. That will be his name: Pal."

Trouble was relieved to hear the name change. "Thank you so much, Miss Gladys. I love you already."

Cheryl paid Mary and thanked her for mentioning at church the information about her pups for sale. Mary and Ginger watched with sadness as Pal sat in Cheryl's car on the lap of his new mom, Gladys. Ginger was especially sad to see one of the pups leaving. She ran back in the house with tears in her eyes and watched through the kitchen window as Cheryl drove away with her cute brown and white fuzzy pup. The date was May 27, 2003.

My first ride in an automobile was new and exciting.

Talking to myself, I said, "*Here I am sitting on my new Mom's lap. I wish she would hold me up so I could see out the window. My real Mom told me there is a big beautiful world outside; I'd like to see it; but I guess I won't see it lying here on my mom's lap! … What a bummer!*"

I heard my new dad Lee say we were going to Cheryl's house first before making the long drive to my new home. After a short drive, I guess we had arrived at Cheryl's house because we all got out of the car. It was good to get out. The instant my Mom placed me on the ground, I ran for the grass at the side of the driveway: boy, did I ever have to go. "Whew! … Now, that's a relief!"

I tried to run around in the grass, but it was too tall, so my Mom picked me up and took me into Cheryl's house. "*Wow, what a neat place: lots of stuff to get into. I sure hope we come back here another time when Dad isn't in such a hurry. I think I would like it here.*"

For some unexplained reason when Lee was talking to me, or as I know him now, Dad, he would call his two grandchildren Uncle and his daughter Cheryl, Aunt Cheryl. Who knows why!

Once inside the house I heard Aunt Cheryl call Uncle Timmy and Uncle Matthew. "Come here, boys; look at the new addition to the family Grandma and Grandpa have. Isn't he cute?"

I began muttering to myself, "*Everyone knows dogs don't have Aunt's and Uncles. And the only Mommy I ever had, stayed behind in that big box on Mary's kitchen floor. I suppose I will just have to get used to the aunt and uncle thing.*"

Cheryl cautioned her boy Tim, saying, "Be careful, Timmy; don't drop Pal; he's just a baby, you know." Uncle

Timmy was lifting me high up in the air, swinging me over his shoulders, and scaring me. I sure was glad Aunt Cheryl made him stop.

Mom and Dad decided it was time for them to make the long drive back home. I was glad to get back in the safety of my Mom's lap and back in the car. Timmy played much too rough for me. I guess if I was all grown up it would have been fun, but I'm not grown up yet; I'm just a little kid.

We rode in the car for a long time and I must have fallen asleep. I heard Dad say we were almost home and that awakened me. I thought to myself, "*We're almost home! I hate to tell you guys this, but I have to go again, and I mean right now! Now the question is: How do I tell them?*" I looked up at Mom's face, but she didn't understand. What do I do? All I could do is cry and squirm around a lot. After a bit Dad must have realized what I was trying to say. I heard him say that he would pull into a grassy area in a motel parking lot to see if I had to go to the potty. Boy, I was glad Dad stopped and just in time!

The car pulled into the driveway and stopped; then Dad spoke to me, not realizing I could understand him, saying, "Well, Pal, I hope you like it here. It's just a small mobile home." Then he added, "They call these houses manufactured homes, but it's our house, and this is your new home, Pal; I welcome you to it!"

I listened to Dad's welcome speech and thought, "*I don't care what people call it: Just so it has a roof and some heat. I sure am going to miss my real mom's warm, soft, fuzzy body. It sure was nice to snuggle close under her chin.*"

Mom carried me into the house and put me down on the soft carpet floor. "Ah, — this is nice, not like the cardboard box I was living in before. And look at this: … lots of stuff for me to play with. I think I'm really going to like this place. Now if I can just find something to eat. I wonder where they keep the food. I think I'll look around and explore a little."

As I was wondering around the house, Dad was unloading my dog things, Aunt Cheryl had given him, from the car.

"I wonder what that big round cushion thing is. It has tall sides on it; I wonder why. He's taking it into the room with the big bed in it. Hmm! … What could that be? He's taken two little dish things from the car and placed them on the kitchen floor. I'll follow him; maybe he will put something like food in them. I'm just curious, you know; that's how we dogs learn. Ah, yes, would you look at that! He *is* putting water in one and something in the other dish. Near as I can tell, it must be dog food. I can tell because the bag he poured the stuff from has a picture of a dog on the front. You know, folks; I'm not as dumb as I look. *Yes! … Yummy! …* I do believe it is puppy food, but it doesn't look like what I had back home. I'm starved though, so I think I'll check it out."

After a bit Dad said to Mom, "Would you look at that, honey? Pal must have been hungry! He ate a little and took a drink of water. At least he knows he won't starve to death or die of thirst in his new home. That was his first lesson, where to find food and water. We're making progress with him already."

Mom usually didn't have much to say about anything, but with a bit of skepticism she said, "Now, if he will just sleep in the new bed Cheryl bought for him."

"According to the book," Dad said, "dogs need a place

they can call their own and his bed beside our bed will be his sleeping and hiding place."

"Sure it will!" Mom said, not sounding very convincing. "I'm going to bed; it has been a long day and I'm tired. You make sure Pal sleeps in his bed. Okay?"

I heard Dad say, "You go ahead, honey, I'll be in shortly. It will be interesting to see how Pal handles his new bed."

So that's what that thing was Dad was carrying in from the car and placed on the bedroom floor beside the big bed. I don't like the looks of this situation.

At this point I didn't want to show any disrespect to Mom and Dad, but I thought, "*Me, sleep in my new bed. You've got to be kidding; I'm sleeping in the big bed with you guys.*"

"Come on, Pal." Dad called. "We're all going to bed now. We have this nice little bed just for you." And with that Dad picked me up and placed me in what he called my new bed.

"I tossed and turned in my new bed, trying to find a comfortable spot to lie down. Ah! … This isn't too bad. Maybe I will like this bed after all." Then I heard Dad get into the big bed and off went the lights.

"Whoa! … Hey, Dad, turn on the lights; it's too dark and scary down here. *Come on, dad*, lights please! If you don't turn on the lights, I'm gonna cry a lot out loud so you can hear me. Come on, Dad, *lights please!*" But the room remained dark. "Okay, guys, you asked for it." And with that, I began to cry and make tiny pup barking sounds that lasted for several minutes.

In a little while I felt Dad's hand reach down from the bed, pick me up, and place me on the pillow between Mom and himself.

"Look, little fellow, you are supposed to sleep in your

nice cozy bed Aunt Cheryl bought for you! Now go to sleep! Tomorrow is a big day. It is May 29, 2003. It is Mom's birthday!" As he was saying that he placed me back in the small bed on the floor.

"If you would just turn on a light, I wouldn't be afraid!" I cried loudly, but again no response from Dad. This should work as I again began quietly crying and whimpering.

"Okay, Pal, you win, but you sleep here between our pillows. If you don't, you might get smashed. Now go to sleep! We'll work on the sleeping arrangements in the morning."

"Good, I'll be able to sleep too, because I can already feel the warmth from Mom's body. I hope she doesn't roll around a lot; I don't want to get smashed." In a short time, I fell asleep. Life is good already.

May 29, 2003. "So today is Mom's birthday."

I knew a new day had arrived as I began to see daylight streaming through the large bedroom window. Another day of curiosity seeking had arrived. I carefully moved from the comfort of my pillow sleeping position to the bottom of the bed. I don't know much yet, but I'm guessing it's not good to wake Mom, especially on her birthday.

After taking several long body stretches at the bottom of the bed, I decided it was time to wake Dad. Why? Because I realized I was hungry. He seemed to be the only one that knew where the food was. But how do you awaken a sleeping giant? … Hmm!

"Hey, Dad," I said, but Dad didn't answer. Of course not! Why would he? He can't hear me. Nevertheless, I continued to talk to myself, "It's been a long time since I had anything to eat. Come on, Dad; wake up! I sure am hungry!" Still no response. "Okay, Dad, you are not going to like this, but I need your attention." Using the best alarm clock I could think of, I crawled on top of Dad's sleeping head.

Like a big fly-swatter, Dad's hand of authority hit me with one mighty swat. I found my body taking several tumbles in the bed.

"Go away, Pal," an annoyed Dad said. "It's not time to get up."

Read on and you will find out I'm not one to give up easily. Slowly I moved close to Dad's ear and began to quietly whine and lick his face with my tongue.

Mom, hearing the commotion quietly said to Dad, "I think my birthday Pal is trying to tell you he is hungry and wants you to get up."

Reinforcing what Mom just said, I screamed, "You got that right, Mom! Tell him again; I don't think he heard you!"

"Honey …."

An irritated Dad cut off Mom, saying. "I heard you the first time. I'm getting up! *Okay?* And I'll get breakfast for *your little birthday friend.*"

A drowsy and nearly awake Dad stumbled his way to the kitchen.

"Okay, Pal, where are you if you are so hungry? … Oh, darn, I guess he is still on the bed."

Dad returned to the bedroom to find me attempting to climb down the bed comforter, trying to reach the floor. "Come on, kid, you belong in the kitchen." With Dad's big hand he picked me up and carried me to the kitchen.

Looking at the empty food dish on the floor, I said, "Now what's the problem, Dad? I still don't see any food in my dish."

Dad decided to make coffee first. Coffee for Dad comes before anything happens in the morning. As he was pouring the water in the coffee maker, he looked at me on the floor, gazing into my empty food dish. Totally frustrated, I had placed my nose in the food dish and began to push it around on the floor. "This dish is a heavy little thing, but sooner or later Dad has to notice it's empty."

Dad did finally notice the dish movement on the floor and said, "You must be really hungry, Pal. I sure hope today was not your usual method of waking me."

Talking to myself, I said, "It's about time you get the hint, Pop! One of these days I'll learn to sit up and point to the dish. Maybe then you'll get the hint faster. Come on, Pop! *Food*, I need food!"

"Okay, Pal, I got the hint. Let's see what kind of dog food we have in your food closet." Dad said under his breath. "Ah-ha! … Here's some dry dog bone biscuit stuff; maybe you can eat this. The box says it has lots of vitamins."

Looking at the box I tried to tell Dad, "I can't eat that stuff, Dad. Look in my mouth; you can see I don't have teeth yet. Come on, Pop, you gotta be smarter than that. Keep looking; I know you have food in that big closet for puppies like me." You probably wonder how I could read the writing on the box. I'm just a little kid, you know. Actually I can't read yet, but I could see the picture on the box.

Anyhow, Dad stopped looking in the closet and went to the dining room table that had the book about Shih Tzu dogs and searched the book for food for baby pups. "Ah, here we go! … Here is the part that's all about feeding your young pups. *Good grief*," he thought out loud. "*These dogs need the same thing humans need: protein, meat, carbohydrates, vitamins from fruits and vegetables, and minerals. Golly, Pal is going to eat healthier than me.*" Still talking to himself, Dad said, "Pal can't eat these big dry biscuits yet; he doesn't have any teeth. Let's see what else is in the closet."

Looking higher in the cupboard, Dad saw a box of another kind of dog food, "We'll try this, Pal. I think you can eat this moist packet of food. It has meat and vegetables! … Yummy! Last night you had the tiny bits of dry puppy food. I think one day I'll give you the dry puppy food and the next day this delicious moist food. You need both kinds for the vitamins and all that other stuff. Besides, they both say they are good for small puppies, and, Pal, you are definitely small."

As Dad stood in the kitchen, reading the dog book, I sat patiently waiting by my new food dish.

"Now you're talking, Dad. Put the good stuff right here in the dish," as I pointed with one foot in my food dish. In a few moments Dad had placed a healthy portion of the soft, moistened food in the food dish.

I sniffed it first to see if it met my high standards before beginning to eat. I remember something my real Mom said. She said to be very careful to sniff the food people try to give you. Sometimes humans give you food that is not good for you to eat. "You don't want to get sick because you ate bad food."

"It's about time! … Lip-smacking good it is! Umm…! This is not bad at all." After a considerable time of slurping and slopping, I devoured most of the packet, leaving a little for a treat later in the morning. Dad, not understanding why I didn't eat everything, reached down to pick up the dish. "Hey, Pop, I'm not finished. I'm saving the rest for later!" I screamed, but of course I knew Dad couldn't hear me, and with that said, I placed my front paw in the dish, preventing him from taking it away.

"Okay, Pal, I can take a hint; I'll leave the dish for now; but you had better finish it in the next few hours or so."

"Sure, Dad, just leave the dish for now. When I'm done, the dish will be clean and you won't even have to wash it."

About 8 AM, a sleepy-eyed Mom appeared on the scene from the bedroom and said to Dad, "How did you make out with our child last night and this morning?"

"He went to sleep finally, but not until I placed him between us on the pillow. He is a persistent little devil. Then this morning, after I fed him, he all but stood on his food dish that still had a little food left in it, as though he was saying, "*It's mine, and I'm still not finished!*"

"Determined little bugger, isn't he?" Mom said, sounding as though she felt that I just might be smarter than Dad.

Mom sat down at the breakfast table and was served coffee by Dad.

"What would you like for breakfast today, honey? Today is your special birthday. You may have anything your heart desires."

"The children have given me the one thing I have wanted for a long, long time: a new best friend!"

Mom looked down at me on the floor, trying to sit up on my hind legs as though begging. "Pal, *you* are my very best friend. I love you so much already!"

"You're right, honey! ... I can see he loves you, and given time, I'm sure I will bond with him also. I think he already knows who loves him and also who gets him stuff."

CHAPTER 3

. . . .

A Doggie Door, What's that?

Dad screamed. "Pal, what are you doing?"

Somewhat frightened by Dad's scream, I stopped and stared at him as though saying, "I have to go someplace and the kitchen floor seems like a good place."

A slightly calmer Dad, realizing I wasn't yet potty trained, said. "Pal, I appreciate your thoughtfulness of going on the kitchen floor rather than on the carpet, but you *must* go to the potty outside."

"But, Dad," I said to myself, standing by the door, looking way up high at the door knob. "I'm just a little guy; I can't reach the knob, you know! What do you expect me to do?"

Dad doesn't know why he talks to me out loud, but he does it all the time. Already, Mom is beginning to wonder about Dad and his dog discussions.

"Hey, Mom," Lee calls Gladys Mom a lot, "I'm going to

the store to get one of those doggie doors for the back door. We have to train Pal to go outside and not on the floor like this."

"And I suppose he will automatically know the little swinging door is for him to get outside." Mom said in a somewhat sarcastic fashion. "Now I guess *I'm supposed* to clean up his mess."

"No, dear, I'll clean it up right now. Please bring me some of today's newspaper? They say if you place a newspaper on the floor by the door, he will understand that is where he is supposed to go to the potty."

"Oh, I see, it's just like you have in your bathroom. You have a newspaper there so you know where to go to the bathroom too! … That must be a male thing."

"Don't get smart, dear! I read the newspaper trick in the dog book." Having said that, Dad placed the funny paper section by the back door and dabbed a tiny bit of my doo-doo on it so I will sniff it and realize that this the place to go.

Dad left for the store to find the doggie door he told Mom about. While Dad was gone I again had to go to the potty. "I guess all the water I drank after I ate is making me need to go so often. Let's see if I can figure out this new potty arrangement. I heard Dad say he is putting newspaper by the back door for me."

Slowly I walked toward the back door and said to myself, "Wow, look at this, a paper that's in color on the floor and with lots of pictures." Sniffing the paper, I decided this must be the place Dad wants me to go. "Gee, I wish I could read; this looks like it must be a very funny newspaper. When I get a little older, maybe Dad will teach me how to read."

In less than half an hour Dad returned with a box that had

the doggie door inside it. Dad said to Mom, "These things are expensive, but I guess it will be worth it if Pal will use it to do his stuff outside."

Mom is amazed that Dad would take on a project like installing a doggie door, and said, "I guess you know you have to cut a hole in the back door for that thing. How are you going to do that? You have never done anything like that before. Did you also buy a new door to replace the old one when you mess it up?"

"Humph! … I'll just get my handy dandy electric saw and show you just how it is done, *ye one of little faith!*"

After about twenty minutes, Dad managed to get the door off the hinges, took it to the back porch, and carefully laid it on the big picnic table. For a change, he decided to read the directions that came with the store-bought doggie door. An hour and a half later he finished the project and hung the back door on its hinges. Satisfied with his fine workmanship, he proudly said to Mom, "See, it's just like the picture on the box. And you thought I couldn't do it."

"Ah, honey! —" Gladys said. "You truly are a genius; you can do anything if you want. But I think you might want to look at the picture on the box again; I think you might have put the doggie door in backwards."

Dad, questioning Mom's statement, glanced at the newly hung back door, "Darn, you're right. Oh, well, that's an easy fix. I'll just take the screws out of the doggie door and put the inside out and the outside in, and then it will work properly."

Dad finished the job again and Mom said to him, "Now it looks like the picture on the box, honey. So I suppose Pal will just jump right through that if he has to go. How are you going to get him to use it, dear?"

"Treats, my dear, promise him treats. The book says that works every time."

A skeptical Mom said, "Sure, I'm sure that will work. Just out of curiosity, what is to keep other critters out of the house? You know, like the stray cats, opossums, and skunks."

By now Dad was sick of her skepticism; but nevertheless, he had to scratch his head as he thought of a solution. "You're right, if the critters realize there is food just inside the door, that could become a problem. I'll have to put up a high wire fence. That way Pal will have his own private run area and the critters won't be able to come inside the house."

Mom agreed with his answer and said, "I sure hope you are right. Pal sure is a bit of trouble, but he is worth it. I love him so much."

"It took some doing, but Dad finally convinced me to use the doggie door by using small moist doggie treats. Now if Dad could just get me to use it for its intended use: going to the potty outside ... The book says you have to be patient and Dad is that, most of the time."

Late in the afternoon, Dad had to go to work, but before he left the house he placed a nightlight in the bedroom near my new doggie bed on the floor. Before he left, he cautioned Mom, saying, "Be sure to turn on the nightlight before you turn out the bedroom light. Hopefully that will satisfy Pal's night fright and keep him sleeping in his bed."

"Sure, dear, but if he cries during the night I'm putting him in my bed."

When I heard what Mom said, I thought, "*That's right, Mom, you do that! That mean old Dad expects me to sleep on the floor all by myself, and I'm not going to do that; you can count on it!"*

I was very content laying on Mom's lap as she rocked me on her living room recliner. She sang old time hymns to me; at least that is what she called them. Then she fell asleep with the TV on. I wonder if Dad knows she sleeps with the TV on. Oh, well, I guess its okay, but I wish she would wake up soon; I have to go outside again.

I began squirming in Mom's lap, "I wonder if I could jump down to the floor; I gotta get down, *now!*" I managed to turn myself around and slide down her leg. Suddenly I slipped and fell the rest of the way to the floor. After I shook off the fall, I ran like the dickens to the kitchen. "Whew! — Just made it! I sniffed around a bit, smelling for my place to go on the newspaper again. How considerate of Dad. I guess that's why Dad left the papers on the floor. If Dad thinks I'm going outside through that little door to go to the potty in the dark night, well I'm not."

When I returned to the living room, Mom had turned off the TV and had gone into her bedroom. "Guess I should go to bed too, but I'm not sleeping in that little doggie bed again! I hope Mom knows that."

Mom called to me, "Come on, Pal, get in your bed. See, your Daddy left a little nightlight on so you won't be in the dark."

I tried to be stubborn, avoiding the little bed, but Mom could see through that, and picked me up and placed me in my bed on the floor. Shortly, Mom turned off the big room light and the room was dark except for the tiny nightlight. As I lay there in the almost dark room, I could see big shadows dancing on the ceiling. "I wonder what that could be! … It looks like … a … a big head with scary eyes. *Mom*, what is that big thing on the ceiling. *Hey, Mom*, help me; I'm scared!" But Mom couldn't hear me.

She must have heard me crying and fussing around in the little bed, because she reached over the edge of the bed, picked me up, and placed me in the big bed on the pillow beside her.

"Wow, that was scary! At last I'm safe from that thing! Thanks, Mom!" I decided to lay beside Mom's head on my back; hoping she would rub my belly. Dad did that yesterday and it felt so good. Suddenly I saw this thing on the ceiling. I just lay there staring at it moving around and around. I couldn't help myself; I began to cry and fuss. Mom reached over and put her big arms around me and looked at me looking at the shadow on the ceiling.

"Pal, are you seeing that shadow on the ceiling?" Mom asked, as she looked up. "I guess that's what you must be seeing. I suppose the fan is blowing the window blind cord and the nightlight below it must be making the shadow dance on the ceiling. I'll turn the fan off." She reached up and pulled the cord to stop the fan. "See, Pal, it stopped dancing. Are you happy now?"

Mom rolled over on her side and didn't even try to rub my belly. "Guess I have to teach her belly rubbing some other time." I looked at the ceiling and the thing was still there, but it wasn't moving. "I guess Mom killed it."

Much later during the night I heard people sounds in the dark house. I didn't like that, but then I thought I heard Dad mumble something, so I was almost sure it was Dad who had come home from work. It was still dark in the bedroom, so I knew it wasn't time to eat or get up. "I suppose he went to bed in the other bedroom. Guess he didn't want to wake Mom. What a nice Dad!"

Hours later there was a small amount of light shining through the window; it was morning at last. Before long Mom got up and went into her bathroom and closed the door. "Hmm! — Wonder what Mom is doing! Think I'll just look around and see what that shiny stuff is on that neat little table beside the bed. … *Wow*, this looks like some neat stuff to play with. I wonder what this could be! … It is bright and shiny, and it makes a kind of ticking noise. I wonder what this leather thingy is that's hanging on it." I began chewing on one of the leather things and immediately spit it out. "Ugh, it's definitely not food! … Ah-ha!" I said, while continuing to search the table top. "Now, this is much better. I don't know what it is, but it looks like it might be candy." I put one long piece of it in my mouth. "Not candy for sure, but it is good to chew on." As I continued to chew on the candy-like thing, the bathroom door opened, and I quickly dropped the chewy like thing. It fell on the floor behind the little table. Later I found out Dad calls the little table a nightstand.

Mom, seeing Pal roaming about the bed said, "Pal, what are you doing? I suppose you are still too small to jump to the floor." She reached over on the bed, picked me up, and placed me on the floor. "There now, Pal, go get your Daddy."

Dad was peacefully sleeping in the other bedroom and was slowly awakened by the sounds of a tiny Pal trying to get his attention. It took awhile, but I finally realized success. Dad reached to the floor and picked me up. "You know, Pal, for a tiny dog you sure do make a lot of noise. Here, Pal, come, lie on the pillow and be quiet; I need a little more sleep. You know, I didn't get home from work until the wee hours of the morning."

As I listened to Dad's story of wanting to sleep, I thought, *"So that was Dad moving around in the house during the night. Sure wish he would say something so I wouldn't think it was a stranger or a burglar."*

The possibility of Dad going back to sleep was again interrupted by a crying Mom in his bedroom doorway. *"Lee,"* when Gladys calls Dad by his name, he knows there is trouble. "I can't find my glasses. I left them on the nightstand, but they're not there."

Realizing the seriousness of the situation Dad said, "Now, Mom, I'm sure they are in your bedroom someplace. You go sit in the living room and I will look for them." As he was saying that, Dad looked straight into my eyes and said, "Pal, do you know where Mom's glasses are?"

Of course there was no answer, but my thoughts were, *"Why are you looking at me, Dad? I don't even know what glasses are! For sure I didn't take them. Remember, I'm just a little puppy!"*

Dad looked all through Mom's bedroom with no luck. Finally he pulled the nightstand away from the wall and there they were. "Hey, honey, I found them behind the nightstand." Picking them up from the floor, Dad found one glass was broken out of the rims. "Well, at least the pieces are here. You must have dropped them when you went to bed."

Mom quickly defended herself, saying, "I know I didn't drop them. I just laid them on top of the nightstand like I always do."

"Hmm! ..." Upon closer inspection Dad noticed the one remaining glass looked like it had been licked or slobbered on. "Pal! … *You did get* your Mom's glasses! Now what will she do? She can't see without glasses. *You are a bad Pal*!"

I stood in the bedroom doorway with my ears drooping and my head lowered in shame, as I listened to Dad's stern scolding. — "*So that's what that thing was I was chewing on. And I thought it was candy. Whoops, I'm sorry, Dad.*"

How to punish a baby dog was the situation Dad was now facing. About all he could do was scold me. "Pal, you have a whole bunch of toys to play with. Don't you *ever* pick up *anything* on the nightstand again? **Do you hear me, Pal**?"

My ears drooped again as Dad continued scolding me, "*I hear you, Dad! I'm right here; you don't have to yell so loud. I promise not to do that again… I think!*"

The ranting continued for a bit, and then Dad said to Mom, "Mom, I'll call the eye doctor today and we'll get you another pair of glasses. Okay? When you go to bed, though, place your glasses high up on the bookcase shelf; that way Pal won't be able to reach them"

"After we go to the eye doctor," Dad continued, "we should stop by the veterinarian and make an appointment to have Pal neutered. The book says if you're having that done, it should be done when the dog is very young."

"But he is so tiny," Mom said with empathy in her voice. "Do we have to, honey?"

"Yes, dear, we do!"

I knew they were talking about me. But I didn't know what a veterinarian was or what *neuter* meant. "I sure wish Mom and Dad would talk words I understand. I don't know what it all means, but I know already I am not going to like it."

CHAPTER 4

. . . .

First Visit to the Veterinarian

Dad made arrangements with Mom's eye doctor to get her new glasses. On the return trip from the eye doctor Dad pulled into an office building that had a sign on it: *Veterinarian.* Only reason I knew what the sign said was that Dad read it. "Veterinarian Office, this is the address that was listed in the phone book. I sure hope they aren't busy; I hate to wait like I do at my doctor's office." Mom waited in the car while Dad took me into the office place.

"Interesting place, I wonder what they do here!" was my thought, as we waited inside the veterinarian office building. *"Sure wish Dad could hear me."* On the far side of the office was a big crazy looking dog that seemed to be trying to pull a little lady out of her chair. *"Look there, Dad; that funny looking bird is calling for help. He wants to get out of this place."* Golly, I wonder what this terrible place does.

It wasn't long until the reception lady told Dad to take me into examining room 2. Dad placed me on the high examination table and stood by me so I wouldn't fall off. This new adventure was beginning to freak me out and I started to squirm around. "Sit still, Pal; the doctor will be here in just a few minutes."

No sooner had Dad said that when the door opened and the lady doctor came into the room. "Good morning, Mr. Drayer. I'm Doctor Robinson and this must be your new dog Pal." Doctor Robinson took control of me by holding me tight and began to gently stroke my coat of shiny fur. That felt good and I calmed immediately, allowing the doctor to begin, what she called, "the examination." She continued brushing my hair and said, "Good morning, Pal, and how are you?"

Questioning myself and wondering if the doctor could understand what I was going to say, I said, "*Why, I'm just fine, … I think. Now if you could just tell me what you are going to do …*" Of course she didn't hear me.

Doctor Robinson was a pretty lady doctor and was one of those touchy feely kinds of people. First she pushed a thing in my bottom; I wasn't too thrilled about that. Then she stuck another thing in my ears, and then she shined a tiny little bright light in my eyes. Finally she squeezed my jaws so hard I had to open my mouth. "Amazing," she said, "he has no teeth."

"*I don't know what doctors do. Apparently they don't know much about little baby pups. I could have told her I don't have teeth; she didn't have to squeeze my jaws like that.*"

Then she laid me on my back, spread my back legs apart, and said, "I can take care of **that** Wednesday morning." I don't know what ***that*** was, but it sounded like I was going to see her again on Wednesday. I wonder what for.

Without saying a thing she scooped me up into her arms and took me to the back room. I guess it's the place they do the things doctor's do. She laid me on a machine thingy and took several pictures of me. I thought I heard her say it was an x-ray machine. She kept saying, "This won't hurt, so just hold still for a second." In a few minutes she took me back to Dad in the waiting room. In her hand she had some picture things she placed on the wall that made light shine through them.

"Bone structure," Dr. Robinson pointed to some picture places and explained to Dad, "looks good except for the hip bones. The hip bone structure is a little thin. It's not a problem now, but later in his life it could become a problem. Later next month, bring him back for his vaccination shots. You will need the vaccination certificates to get him licensed. I thank you, Pal, for being a nice gentleman doggie. Mr. Drayer, bring him in on Wednesday at about 8 am. You must leave him here for the day and pick him up about 5 pm. I'll give you instructions about how to take care of him at that time. Pal, you sure are a cute little fellow. Here, Pal, is a good doggie treat, just for you."

I gave Dr. Robinson a nasty stare as though saying, "The treat is good, but that won't make me like this place any better."

"X-rays, so that's how they can see through your skin and fur. For a cute little fellow I sure am learning a lot, but I still don't know what ***that*** is. Maybe Dad will tell me later."

Dad and Mom don't talk much to each other, but when they do, I like to listen. This evening was no exception. I was roaming around the living room trying to play with the squeaky play toy Aunt Cheryl gave me. I actually wanted Dad to play with me, but he was busy reading the newspaper and ignored me completely. The silence was broken by Dad talking to Mom. "I sure am glad I'm off work for the next few days. After they do the operation Wednesday, Pal has to stay at the clinic all day."

"Really?" Mom said. "Why?"

Dad tried to explain, "You know what they do when they neuter a male dog. Right? I guess they have to stitch him up, and they will keep him to make sure he doesn't have complications or start bleeding. If it looks okay, I can pick him up before they close for the night."

"Oh, dear, that sounds so brutal." Mom said.

"Well, my dear, that's why you have it done when they are so young."

The dinner Mom was cooking smelled so good to me, but Dad would never give me anything from the table. As Mom and Dad ate their dinner, I took my usual begging place beside the table. I stood by the table on my hind legs with my front paws extended out ready to accept any food, but there was nothing, not even from Mom. Oh, sure, every once in awhile some tiny piece of food would miss Dad's mouth, falling to the floor. But that was it, nothing of significance. Ha! … And you thought I didn't know big words. Instead I had to eat the stuff in those little dog food packets. Someday I'll be big enough to sit at the table and eat their stuff. I can hardly wait.

All evening I was thinking about Wednesday and the doctor thing. Eventually I went into Dad's bedroom and found one of his slippers on the floor. For some reason I found it a comfort to me to rest my head on his slippers. I suppose I felt safer if I could smell the stinky scent of Dad's feet. I know that's gross, but I'm a dog.

"I wonder where Pal is." Dad said as he looked toward Mom in her recliner who was nearly asleep. "Surely he didn't go outside by himself. I wonder if he is in your bedroom, getting into trouble again." Dad got up from his recliner and checked in Mom's bedroom, but no Pal. "Where could he be?"

"Hey, Dad, I'm in here. Come in your bedroom; I want to talk to you!" yelled Pal, but Dad didn't come. Why would he come? He can't hear me.

I could hear Dad looking all over the house and finally he came into his room. "There you are! … What are you doing in here all by yourself?"

I tried to look as sad as I could. I turned my face up and looked at him with my big black teary eyes, as though saying, "*We need to talk, Dad.*"

It was good to have him reach down and pick me up with his big hands and lay me on his bed on my back. Dad did understand what I wanted to know.

He began to stroke my belly which made me want to purr like a kitten. But thank goodness, I'm not a cat. As he rubbed my belly, he began to tell me what I wanted to know about Wednesday.

"Day after tomorrow, Pal, you and I are going back to see the nice lady doctor. She is going to take you in the back room and put you on, what they call, an operating table. The other lady that is back there will give you something to make you sleep. After they are sure you are sleeping, they will spread your back legs apart, and the lady doctor will make a tiny cut and remove these two tiny little things."

In a very loud voice, never before heard from a dog, I screamed ...*"**They're going to do what?**"*

Surprised by what I just said, Dad said, "That is what neutering is! —" After a long pause Dad said, "I must be dreaming, Pal. Did I just hear you say, '*They're going to do what?'*"

"I think I heard myself say it, Dad, but you and I know dogs can't talk out loud, so I know you didn't hear that."

"But I did, Pal! ... I know that is what you said. ... Come on, say something else." Better yet, go into the bathroom and say something to me. I want to be sure I'm not losing my mind.

Hopping off the bed, I did as Dad asked, and then spoke to him from the bathroom in a loud voice, "**Dad, can you hear me now? It's Pal!**"

"Incredible, Pal! ... You really can talk and I can hear your voice."

When I came back in the bedroom, I jumped back on the bed. "When I called you from the bathroom, I called loud enough for Mom in the living room to hear me also, but she didn't hear. That makes the two of us very special communicators. ... Wow, another big word; I'm gettin' good at this talkin' stuff."

"Just remember, no other human in the whole world will be able to hear me talk except you, so don't try to get rich off my communication voice."

Now what was I saying before the voice revelation happened? "Oh, yeah, Dad, why would the doctor cut me like you said?"

In spite of what I told Dad, he still wanted to call Mom and tell her that I could talk, but then he thought she would think him crazier than usual.

A stunned Dad tried to explain neutering to me as best he could. "You remember, Pal, when we watch the Price Is Right in the morning, Bob Barker always ends the show saying, Remember to have your pets spayed or neutered to control the pet population."

"So-o ...."

Dad said, "If everybody in the world did that there would not be so many homeless dogs and cats. When you grow up you won't be able to make puppies like some dog did with Lady your mother."

After thinking about what Dad said, I replied, "Yeah, but then I wouldn't be here with you and Mom! Right?"

Dad was unwilling to go on with the neuter conversation, so he said, "Some day when you grow up, Pal, you will understand."

"Dad, are you sure the lady doctor won't hurt me?"

"Yes, Pal, I'm sure. You won't feel a thing."

Bewildered by the new talking Pal, Dad said, "Come, Pal, it's about time for bed and you need to go outside! Okay?"

"I suppose you expect me to use the little swinging door you made."

"Yes, Pal, I do. I'll go through the big door and you follow me through your little door. Okay? If you do that right, I'll give you a special treat: some vanilla ice cream."

Always up to new challenges, especially for treats, I agreed to try it, even though I didn't know what ice cream was. With considerable coaxing by Dad, I finally went through Dad's little swinging door. "Okay, Dad, now that I'm out here, what am I supposed to do?"

"This is where you do your doo-doo business, Pal, or whatever you need to do before you go to bed. That way you won't make a mess in the house during the night like you have been lately."

"But, Dad, in case you haven't noticed, there aren't any papers on the cement floor out here like there are in the house for me to go on."

Swinging his arms around as though showing me the entire back yard, Dad said, "I know, Pal, I want you to think of this big grassy area in the back yard as your big doo-doo newspaper. Go any place you want. Isn't it great, Pal, your own big doo-doo newspaper yard? But it isn't paper; it is nice soft grass. Try it, Pal, you'll like it." And I did!

I knew the time had come for me to quit playing in the yard when Dad said, "Okay, Pal, it is time for bed. In the house you go, but go in through the little swinging door. I want to make sure you know it's a two-way door. You know, you can go outside from inside and back into the house through the little door. Okay?"

"I'll try to do it, but it is a big step up for me to reach the little door thingy." With two tries, I was able to get inside. As I accomplished the task and was back in the kitchen I said to Dad, "Don't forget, Dad, you promised a treat."

For the next hour or so we both sat in Dad's big recliner and watched the Tonight show. Mom had already gone to bed. "Hey, Dad," I said. "how come you and Mom sleep in different bedrooms?"

"Well, it's like this, Pal. Several years ago Mom got tired of me poking her during the night, waking her out of a deep sleep. Each time I did that I said, 'Mom, you're snoring again; roll over and stop it!'"

To which she said, "I don't snore. Stop poking me; you know you grit your teeth in your sleep too."

"Apparently, Pal, she was right because my dentist confirmed my front teeth were ground down considerably."

"So, what did you do, Dad?"

"After several heated discussions about the matter, I decided that since we have an extra smaller bedroom, why not use it. I left Mom with the big bedroom and the bigger bath, and I went to my smaller bedroom and bath. Now both of us sleep much better. Does that answer your question, little fellow?"

"Sure does." Satisfied with the answer I said, "But where should I sleep? I like sleeping between both of you in the big bed."

"Pal, you are supposed to sleep in your own bed on the floor. However, it appears you are not going to use it, so you can sleep with either Mom or me. The choice is yours. Let's go to bed; I have a busy day tomorrow."

After considerable thought, I said, "Tonight, Dad, I would like to sleep with you. But when you go to work and leave Mom and me alone, I have decided I will be sleeping in her room. To be honest, Dad, sleeping in the dark scares me. When I was on the floor in that little bed, I thought I saw scary things dancing on the ceiling. Mom showed me it was only a shadow, but I was afraid anyhow."

Trying to reassure me, Dad said, "Well, Pal, there is nobody in the house except you, me, and Mom! Okay?"

It wasn't long before Dad was in his bed. He left the ceiling fan running slowly, creating a cool breeze that felt so good softly blowing on me. He told me he can't sleep unless there is air circulating. The fan also has a light chain and after he said, "Good night, Pal, go to sleep." he pulled the chain and the light went out with no scary shadows dancing on the ceiling.

I think it is strange that Dad sleeps on his belly, just like me. Most of the time I sleep on my belly too, but sometimes I like to lay on my back with my legs spread apart, allowing the cool breeze to cool my bottom side.

"I don't know why Dad has a pillow because he only uses a tiny corner of it, leaving the whole top part for me to sleep on."

Tonight I decided to curl up on the pillow above Dad's head. It felt good to know he was close, because he has a nice Dad scent that I can smell. I know that sounds dumb, but we dogs have sensitive noses and sniffing is one way of telling who is with us in the dark.

After a bit Dad stopped tossing around on the bed, looking for his perfect spot to rest his head. The only sound in the room now was that of the slowly whirling ceiling fan.

"Dad," I said sounding a little puzzled. "You said tomorrow you are going to have a busy day."

"That's right, Pal."

"Dad, what are you going to do?"

"Pal, if you must know, I have some wire fence and I'm going to build a fence around a small area of the back yard. That will be your own protected run area."

"Why?"

"Because I don't want you running away, and I don't want wild critters coming through the doggie door. Now go to sleep!"

"Dad?"

"Hush, Pal, go to sleep!" And with that said he placed his hand on my back and softly stroked it a few times.

"I think Dad and I are beginning to bond. I don't know

what that means, but I think he is beginning to love me like Mom does."

I don't know what time it was, but it was late when Dad began to grind his teeth and tossed around like a crazy person on the bed. I was glad I was on the pillow. Most of the covers he had on him fell to the floor. To protect myself I moved to the other pillow just to be safe. It's no wonder Mom doesn't want him in her bed. Mom never moves once she goes to sleep.

Sure enough, next morning Dad was out in the back yard pounding the posts into the ground to support the fence. The fence looked high enough to keep me in my area forever. When he finished, he looked at me and said, "Let's see you try jumping over that high, three foot fence. Now, the only problem I have is how to close the space between the house and the utility shed. I'll have to make some kind of gate."

That said, he sat down by the picnic table and began to talk to himself. Dads do that a lot, you know! "Gee, I wonder if I still have a piece of plywood wide enough to fill that space! … Hmm." It wasn't long until almost everything in the storage shed was on the patio cement floor outside the shed.

"Sure enough, Pal, this should do it." And out came a big piece of plywood that would more than fill the space. "I'll just get my handy dandy electric saw and cut this down to the right size."

When I heard that electric saw start screaming, I ran into the house. High pitched noises like that hurt my ears. When Dad finished sawing, I came outside again and said, "You know, Dad, when you are going to make a screaming noise like that, warn me so I can cover my ears. That really hurts."

Dad said he was sorry. He said he remembered reading in the Shih Tzu book where it said my breed was extremely sensitive to loud, high pitched noises.

After considerable effort, the board almost fit perfectly; at least that's what he said, but how to hold it in place ... He went rummaging through more stuff in the shed and found two plastic U shape tracks. Dad decided that if they are screwed to the house wall and the shed wall, the board would fit just right. Only problem, "Darn, the board is about an inch too wide; I'll have to saw some more off the sides. Pal, go in the house; I'm going to run the saw again."

When I went outside again, sure enough Dad had the board in place and I had a safe place to run around: No fear of critters invading my run area now.

It was Wednesday morning, July 4, 2003. Dad had not forgotten he was supposed to take me to see the lady doctor at the veterinarian place. I thought this was not going to be a fun thing, so I decided to hide. I heard him calling. "Maybe he will just give up trying to find me. No such luck though, he found me in Mom's bathroom, hiding behind that big white thing she sits on."

"Come on, Pal, we have to go." He said.

"No, Dad, *we* don't have to go. *You* go without me!"

Dad was trying to teach me things by making promises. "After this is over, I will give you a bigger than usual treat of ice cream tonight. Now come on!" As good as that sounded, I continued to hide, but with his long arms he reached down and scooped me up and off we went.

Some time in the afternoon I woke up in the lady doctor's back room and realized I was in the care of two very nice ladies. When they saw I was squirming around, they picked me up, held me tight, and gently rubbed my belly. To my surprise I had no pain from whatever they did to me while I slept. Little did I know they had given me medicine that caused the pain to go away?

The problem with situations like this is the fear you have. The fear is because you really don't understand what is going to happen. I definitely was afraid, but as it turned out, it wasn't bad after all. Now, if Dad will keep his promise about the ice cream treat, I'll be happy.

Late that afternoon Dad came as promised. He picked me up and held me close to his face, looking at my belly. I suppose he was looking to see what the doctor had done. "Pal, you are a new man now. It looks like she did a good job fixing you. Dr. Robinson gave me some medicine for you to take so you don't get an infection. Now, Pal, it's time to come home."

While Dad was holding me close to his head, I whispered, "You didn't forget about the ice cream treat, did you?"

Whispering back, Dad said, "No, Pal, I didn't forget."

After he paid the lady, she reminded him to come back in two weeks for a check up and some vaccinations. He made the appointment and we went home. It looks like I'm going to be coming here often.

On the drive home I said to Dad, "I'm sure glad you came when you did. I thought I was going to be staying at that awful place all night. Dr. Robinson and the other two ladies at the clinic were getting ready to go home for the night. She told me if you didn't come soon, I would have to stay there all night. I don't know what those other dogs did, but they were not happy. They were barking and crying all day. That would have driven me nuts if I had to hear that all night."

CHAPTER 5

. . . .

I Was a Really Bad Boy Again!

A frustrated Dad became harsh with Mom as he said, "Honey, how many times have I told you to put your glasses on the bookshelf when you go to bed? Pal is growing up and he is curious about everything within his reach. You know he feels the nightstand is his territory too. He has teeth now and has chewed and broken both lenses *and* the frames. They are totally destroyed. Now you have no glasses until the optometrists can make you a new pair."

"I'm sorry, honey, but I thought I did put them up high last night." Mom said while fighting back tears of sorrow.

Dad placed the pieces in his hand as he looked for me. I overheard the heated discussion with Mom and went hiding in Dad's bedroom. This time Dad went looking for me in his bedroom first. Unfortunately, he found me hiding in the corner beside his bed. "Pal, you should be ashamed of yourself.

Look at this!" Dad said, holding the broken pieces close to my face. "How is Mom ever going to see? You chewed the glasses and broke both of them, and you chewed the frames too! It's going to cost me a lot of money to replace them. It is a good thing you aren't getting an allowance; I'd take it away from you for a year."

"You would give me an allowance, Dad?"

"Don't get smart, Pal! I should paddle you, but I won't. When I'm not here, Mom won't be able to see to get food for you. You'll just have to go hungry until I get home from work. That will be punishment enough for now. Oh … and by the way, I won't give you treats either. ***You've really been a bad dog this time!"***

Time has a way of healing a dog's instinct to chew on everything in sight. Several of the wooden snack trays have teeth marks from my newly forming teeth. That doesn't seem to bother Dad much as long as I don't eat Mom's glasses. Yes, I have chew toys, but "it's a lot more fun chewing the furniture. Did I mention it helps my new teeth grow through the gums? Besides, the furniture has a better flavor than those dumb chew toys."

"You know, Dad," I said, "I think I was born in April. Right?"

"That's right, Pal, April 9, 2003, to be exact," Dad said, wondering where the conversation was going.

"Mom and I were watching TV the other day and a lady had a dog on the TV that was having a birthday. Would you believe it, she said she was having a birthday party for her little dog friend that was only one year old."

"Pal, you and Mom are watching way too much TV."

"Well, Mom likes it and I like it too. Anyhow, the TV lady said she was having ice cream and cake and placed a big candle on the cake. Why, she even put a birthday hat on the little dog's head. Best of all she gave the dog a birthday present all wrapped in pretty paper."

Dad could see I was hinting about my desire to have a birthday party. Clearly the conversation wouldn't end unless there was some kind of party agreement. "Pal, the only cake you may have is a piece of plain white cake. If Mom has a single candle, I'll light it and put it on top of the cake; but you have to make a wish and blow out the lighted candle first. Do you have a problem with that?"

"Ah … yes, maybe just a little one, Dad."

"What's that?"

"I don't think I can blow the lighted candle out … I don't have a blower like you."

"Okay, Pal, Mom and I will do that for you, but you have to make a wish first. If you don't make the wish before blowing the candle out, the wish won't come true. Oh, and if you want, your present will be a great big biscuit wrapped up in pretty, shiny red and gold colored paper. I'm sorry, Pal, I shouldn't have told you what the present was going to be; it spoils the surprise."

Quickly I had to respond to the obvious and I said, "Why not, Dad, that's about all it could be."

I was thinking about the candle thing and said, "So, Dad, what's a wish?"

Dad had to think real hard before answering that question. "I know how to explain it to a person, but you are not a person. Let me think …. Suppose you wanted a little brother or a sister. You would make a wish and say, 'I wish for a new friend like a brother or a sister. Okay?'"

I looked straight into Dad's eyes and exclaimed, "Oh, I get it, Dad, a wish is to want something that is never going to happen in a million years! Right?"

"You got that right, Pal. One of you is quite enough. But if you want a party, Pal, we will have it for you next week on your birthday."

"Thanks, Dad."

Sure enough, the next week Mom baked a small white cake. She put white icing on it and placed the only birthday candle she could find on top, just like Dad promised. With the candle lit, Dad and Mom came in the dining room singing *Happy Birthday* just like they did on TV. It was a happy day for me. Dad placed me on a chair by the dining room table, and as I sat up Dad said to me, "Make a wish, Pal, and then blow out the candle." He took some pictures and I tried to smile, but we all know dogs can't smile; we don't have smile lips. Anyhow, like I said before, dogs can't blow out candles either. Not a problem, Dad and Mom did that for me.

Later after all the birthday celebration was over, Dad and I were out back alone and I asked him a question. "Dad, I'm a little confused. Mom had a big five candle on the cake. I thought I am just one year old. Right?"

"Pal, you are just one today. I didn't think you would notice the number five candle. I went to the store to get a number one candle, but they didn't have any. The only one Mom had in the cupboard was the five. She doesn't know you can count so she used the only one she had. It was a lighted candle, and you made a wish, and we blew it out, and that's all that counts."

The wish was another thing. The only present I wished for

was the thing in the brown wrapper Mom was eating earlier while she was sitting in her chair watching TV. I wanted some of that. But when Dad saw me eyeing the brown wrapper thing, he told me the brown wrapper thing would make me sick. Instead he placed a small piece of cake on the floor in a paper dish along with a tiny bite of vanilla ice cream, and I ate it all.

Then I thought, "*That sure was good. Now if I can just find out where Mom left that brown wrapper thing she was eating.*"

Dad had gone to bed early so it was just Mom and me. "Come to bed, Pal." Mom said from her bedroom.

By now I could jump in the bed by myself. I was all grown up and didn't need help for stuff like that. Besides, as usual, I had to go outside first before going to bed. I wanted to say to Mom, "In a minute," but I know she couldn't hear me. Only Dad can hear, and he was already in his room, leaving me all alone in the dark living room. I went out to the potty all by myself. I know it's dark and spooky outside at night, but I had to go and I did.

Back in the house I began to wonder where Mom could have put that big brown wrapper thing she was eating before she went to bed. I looked everyplace. It was dark, but I'm a dog and I can see in the dark better than people can. I searched and searched and finally I found it on the little table beside Mom's big recliner chair. Since I have no fingers, I had to put the wrapper in my mouth and try to chew it open. Still I couldn't get to the good stuff though. I jumped to the floor with it in my mouth. "Yummy! ... It smells so good!" With my paws and my teeth I managed to get the paper off. "*Me, oh, my*! This is *sooo good!* No wonder Mom tries to hide it from me." Mom only left a few pieces, so it didn't take long for me to finish it off. While still licking my mouth with my tongue, I jumped into her bed.

My usual place in her bed is with my head on the pillow close to her head. I continued licking my mouth, still enjoying the last scent of whatever it was I ate, when Mom said, "Pal, stop licking your lips and go to sleep!" Fortunately she couldn't smell what I had eaten. Actually, Dad said Mom can't smell anything anymore. That is good, because if she could smell, she would have known exactly what I ate.

Morning came early for me. My stomach was making all kinds of strange sounds. Mom was still asleep, but I jumped down and ran to the living room. Dad was up and wondered why I was walking around on the carpet, coughing and gagging so much. It didn't take long for him to know why. I began to heave everything in my stomach onto the carpet.

Dad tried to be sympathetic and said, "I guess we shouldn't have given you the cake last night before bed." I continued slowly walking around gagging up whatever was left in my stomach. Dad came in with a roll of paper towels and began cleaning up the mess when he spotted the remains of the brown wrapper left on the floor by Mom's recliner.

In a not so sympathetic tone Dad said, "Pal, you got up during the night and ate Mom's Hershey Bar, didn't you?"

Not denying it, I said, "Is that what that was? It was so good going down, but it sure is awful coming up." Without saying any more I immediately ran outside and began having awful stuff coming from my other end.

Dad came out to see what was happening to me. He gets angry with me sometimes, but if I am in trouble, he is right by my side. "Pal, I think I had better take you to the vet's office as soon as they open."

By now my rear end began to hurt from going so much. I was still gagging, trying to throw up, but there was nothing left to throw. Frankly, I didn't care what Dad was going to do. "Just get me over this, Dad; I promise never to do that again."

Reassuring me, Dad said, "Mrs. Robinson at the vet place will give you something to get you better, but your Mom will never forgive you for eating her Hershey Bar. Chocolate is the one candy she craves and you ate hers. *Shame on you, Pal!* Chocolate is one thing dogs should never have and now you know the reason why."

Chapter 6

Mirror on the Wall, Is That Me?

Time has a way of making changes a dog can hardly notice. Dad said I have changed, but I don't know how. The reason I don't know is I can't get up high enough to see in a mirror. One time I decided to ask Dad to lift me up so I could see myself in his bathroom mirror.

His response was, "So you want to see who is causing all the trouble, huh?"

"Me cause trouble? I can't help it if you and Mom leave all the neat stuff lying around for me to get into. I'm just a curious little puppy, remember?" I suppose I can't say that any longer. I am getting a bit older, ya know.

After a brief pause, I said, "No, Dad, really, I do wonder what I look like. I don't know if I'm a big dog or a tiny little one. I hope I'm not one of those great big dogs like I saw at the veterinarian's place. Why, I don't even know if I'm pretty or ugly."

"Okay, Pal, come into the bathroom …" Dad paused.

"Oh, I get it. You're going to trick me, then close the door with me inside. No, Dad! … I don't need a bath." I'm on to Dad's tricks by now when it comes time for a doggie bath.

"No, Pal, it's no trick. You asked to see yourself and the mirror is here in the bathroom. Come, I'll pick you up so you can see for yourself." Having said that, Dad reached down and lifted me up to the sink top.

Amazed, I looked at myself in the mirror. "Is that really me, Dad?"

"Do you see another dog here?"

"But, Dad, I thought I would be bigger than that dog in the picture."

"Interesting," Dad said. "That is not a picture, Pal; that's you. It's an image or a reflection of whoever is facing the mirror."

"But, Dad, I've watched Mom looking into her mirror, and when she is done looking into it, there is painted stuff on her face. Does she paint the reflection?"

Clearly it is becoming more of a problem for Dad to try to explain the mirror image so Dad ignored the Mom thing. "Pal, did you think you looked like that?"

"Not really. I remember somebody saying I was such a cute brown and white puppy. I'm not brown and white at all."

Dad tried to explain. "Pal, you are getting older now; you're fully grown up. In people years you are more than seven years old. Your hair color is changing to a tan and cream color. Hair color changes when you get older."

Quick to respond, I said, "Is that what is happening to you? You're old too and your hair has turned really white."

Uncomfortable with the direction of the conversation, Dad said, "I think you have seen enough of the little trouble maker. But nevertheless, as some say, you are a cute little devil."

Appreciating the compliment, I said, "Yeah, now that I've seen myself, I am kind of cute."

Dad placed me on the floor, and as I walked away, Dad said, "Pal, I made an appointment for you to get a haircut tomorrow morning."

Mom was listening to the one sided conversation Dad and I were having from her living room recliner. "Dad, you are talking to Pal as though he can understand everything you say. You do know he is a dog, don't you?"

"I know you think I'm a little crazy, but how do you know he doesn't understand what I say?" Dad said, trying to justify the appearance of talking to me.

Upon hearing Dad say, "Haircut!" I turned and gave him that hateful staring look, reminiscent of my last visit to the haircut lady.

"Come on, Pal, I think you and I need to go outside." He wants to hear my reason for the nasty look. Dad learned if he and I were going to have lengthy conversations, they needed to be held outside, away from Mom's ears.

I enjoy lying in the grass, sunbathing, so I obeyed Dad like the cute little devil he said I was.

Once outside, Dad said. "What's with the stare you gave me in the house, Pal? You do like the lady that cuts your hair, don't you?"

"She's okay, but the floor at her place is covered with hair from all the other dogs she clips. Do you know how many fleas might be living in that stuff? And then she gives me a bath before she cuts my hair and another bath when she is done. Frankly, Dad, one bath would be more than enough. But the thing I really hate most is; she places me in a cage after she washes my hair and turns on a big hurricane-like fan to dry me. There's no way to escape it. How would you like it if the barber did that to you after you get a haircut? You wouldn't; I know you wouldn't — for sure. You would never go back to the same barber again."

A determined Dad said, "Tomorrow you're going to get a haircut, Pal, like it or not. I'll check around and try to find a different pet groomer that doesn't use the cage dryer thing. Better yet, I'll talk to the lady and ask her not to place you in the dryer cage. I'm sure she will understand."

As promised, Dad took me the next day to the, as he calls it, beauty shop. The lady that gives me a haircut calls the shop, *Gerianne's Pet Styling Salon.* It doesn't matter what you call it; I hate going there.

Dad did keep his promise to talk to Gerianne about not drying my hair in the cage with the hurricane dryer after the two baths. She said she could use a hand held hair blower if that would be better. She told Dad, "Some dogs do become extremely upset when I use the cage dryer."

After she told Dad that, it made my body stop shaking. "I thank you, lady."

Dad came back to rescue me in about an hour and Mom was with him. We must be going for a ride in the car.

Usually when the wheels of the car turn, Dad would take Mom and me along for the ride. Mom appreciated it and so did I. Mom would sit in her seat and I would sit on the center arm rest. Wow! … It doesn't get better than this. Sometimes Dad would just drive us around with no particular place in mind. That was fun for me because I knew I wouldn't have to wait in the car alone while they both went in the stores shopping.

Mom would look out the front window and exclaim, "Look, Honey, see how beautiful the blue sky is and the pretty clouds." That statement was always followed by a comment about the beautiful fluffy white clouds. She would say, "God is so good to us, giving us such pretty scenery to look at. I wonder how we get rain out of those pretty white clouds."

Dad would then go through the whole process of what causes rain to come down from the clouds. "Mom," he would say. "the clouds are where the rain comes from. When each of the billions of tiny little water droplets in the clouds gets heavy enough, they begin to fall as rain. The air pressure on earth has to be just right for that to work, however. If the air temperature is very cold, instead of rain, you get snow." And he would go on and on, explaining that if the rain begins falling and there are severe updrafts, the rain is pushed back up very high into the sky, causing the rain to freeze. A single little drop of rain might be pushed high many times, re-freezing it over and over each time. The result of that is hail. When finished, he would say, "Now, Mom, do you understand why it rains?"

Mom would say, "Uh-huh! … But how do you know all that?"

Dad would look at me laying quietly in Mom's lap and say, "I don't know how I know, but it sounds good! *Right,* Pal?"

Mom would always get the last word on the subject, saying,

"I know how it rains and snows: God says rain, or God says snow, and it does." Who's going to argue with that?

CHAPTER 7

A Thanksgiving Trip Is Planned

It was nearly Thanksgiving. The only reason I knew that it was, I heard Mom and Dad say so. Anyhow, the discussion between the two of them was, should they fly or drive to visit their son Gary in Pennsylvania. If they flew, they talked about placing me in a kennel for a few days. If they drove, they would take me along in the car. The real question was, if they drove, would I behave on the long two day drive to Gary's house?

When I was alone with Dad, I said, "Dad, do you remember a long time ago when you and Mom went to visit her friend in Alabama?"

"Yes, Pal, I remember. We placed you in that nice kennel way out in the country. When we got home from the visit, we found you in the arms of the lady that owned the place.

She said she liked you so much she kept you in her house the whole week we were away."

With a somewhat irritated voice I said, "Now, Dad, it's time I tell you the rest of the story."

Dad said, "Is this going to be one of those Paul Harvey, 'rest of the story' things?"

"Well, sort of. The night you left me at that awful place, I cried so much and made such a big fuss, when the lady came out to check on all her visiting dogs, I guess she felt sorry for me. She picked me up with her big soft hands and held me close to her face. Remember, back then I was just a wee, tiny puppy. When she held me close like that, I kissed her face over and over. I suppose it was love at first sight and she took me into her house and placed me in her bed. Remember, Dad, I was a cute little fellow back then. Anyhow, her husband didn't want me in his bed, but she overruled and I was with that nice lady until you and Mom came back for me."

"The lady was nice, but the place was terrible. There were rows and rows of big cages. Each cage had a place where you could come in out of the sun and the rain. And each one had a long space to run outside, but I was still inside a big cage."

"But, Pal, that's the way a good kennel is built."

"I don't care; please don't put me there again. I'll be good on the long drive to Pennsylvania in the car! I promise!"

"No, Pal, I will never again place you in a kennel. Mom and I made that decision after we picked you up way back then. If we can't get a dog sitter to watch you at our house, we won't go away. I promise."

Dad's biggest concern was would I behave when they stayed in a motel overnight along the way. Dad said most motels would not allow pets of any kind and especially, a barking dog. "Dad, have you ever heard me do an all out bark?"

Dad thought for a moment and had to admit, "No, Pal, I haven't. Can you bark?"

"What kind of question is that, Dad? Certainly I can bark if I have to, but nothin' ever happens around here to make me want to."

"I was thinking: because you can speak, that might have taken away your ability to bark."

Exasperated, I said, "God gave me a bark and a talk voice; what do you think of that?"

"For me, having you to talk to is a blessing, most of the time. I'm sorry I asked."

Mom and Dad spent the evening packing suitcases. I did my best to help Mom pack hers, but she didn't seem to appreciate it. I kept reminding her I was going along by hopping into her suitcase and hiding under her nicely folded clothes. "Look, Pal," Mom said, as she pulled me out of her neatly packed suitcase, "I know you are going along, but you have to stay out of my clothes. Now, go pester your Dad." And I did.

Dad had his big suitcase on his bed also. "Dad, are you sure you are taking me along?" Having said that, I hopped into his suitcase too, but Dad wasn't so gentle. With one hand he picked me up and dropped me on the floor.

Having done that, he said, "Yes, Pal, you are going along, but if you don't behave, I might have second thoughts about it. Now, go play with your toys"

The car was loaded with all kinds of stuff in the trunk. We were finally backing out of the driveway, headed for

Pennsylvania. Mom and Dad were in the front seat with me on the front center console looking out. What a picture we were as we left the house in Mom's new car. Dad bought it just a few weeks earlier, but Mom said it was hers.

It was hard for me to understand that part, because several weeks before, Dad had taken Mom to the drivers license place so she could get an identification card that looks like a drivers license, but isn't. Dad and Mom talked about her safe driving ability. Mom was becoming confused as Dad drove her around on the well-known local roads. They both decided it was time for her to stop driving and that was the end of her many years of driving an automobile. Mom never argued about losing her driving license. Nevertheless, she said it was still her new car.

As we traveled north along the interstate, we would stop when Mom said she had to go to the potty. Dad would attach my leash to my collar and the three of us would head for the rest stop potty place. Dad saw that Mom got to the right place, and then he took me to the edge of the woods to do my thing. I would always go even though sometimes I didn't have to. Then he would take me along into his potty place. I wonder if the people that build those little rest stop buildings would make one with a little white potty low enough so we dogs could use them. I hate roaming in the grass, sniffing for a clean place to go. I'm a clean freak, you know!

Along the way we stopped at a motel. At least that's what Dad called it. He told Mom to hold me in her lap while he checked for a room. She told me some motels won't allow dogs, so I had to hide. Dad came out happily holding a room key in the air as he approached the car. When he got in the car, Mom said, "Did they ask about a pet?"

Not one to lie, honest Dad said, "Yes, but they said it

would be okay for an extra five dollars added to the room rate."

"Good," Mom said. "Now we won't have to hide Pal."

The room was nice with two beds, one for me and one for Mom and Dad. That's not the way it worked out however; I slept with Mom in her bed and Dad slept in the other bed.

Mom stayed with me in the room while Dad went out to get food for the three of us. Unfortunately he had brought my food and water dish along and I had to eat my usual dog food stuff. *What a bummer!*

The next day we arrived in Gary's hometown of Souderton, Pennsylvania. As we drove around looking for Gary's house, I noticed the houses were big, two and three story houses — not the little kind we have back home. I thought everyone lived in little places like what Dad called manufactured houses. He eventually found Gary's house. Pulling into the driveway, he said, "We're here, Pal." Looking out the front window of the car, I saw this really big house with a high iron fence beside the house. Inside the fence was a big, I mean a big, dog barking. Dad sensed my fear and said, "Its okay, Pal; he stays outside all the time. Let's see if Gary is home."

Mom talks about her youngest son all the time. She is so proud of him. Her little boy is now almost fifty, but he is still her little boy. Oh, well, Dad says I'm his little boy too. I suppose everyone has a little someone.

The front door opened and out came Gary hugging and kissing Mom and Dad. It was so mushy. Finally Dad introduced me to Gary. He picked me up and said, "Welcome to my little house."

"*Wow*," I thought. "*Little house, I think not.*"

We all went inside and I immediately began checking out

the place that Gary called his little house. It wasn't long until Gary's three girls came home. Gary introduced me to each of them. "Girls, this is Pal, Mom and Dad's newest child." Picking me up and holding me to his chest, he said, "Pal, meet my girls, Christiana, Megan, and Becky."

Immediately an excited Megan said to Gary, "Oh, Daddy, can't I have a little one like Pal to live in our house."

"*Megan*," Gary said. "We have talked about that many times and the answer is still *no!*"

"*But, Dad, why not?*"

"No, Megan, enjoy Pal for the week he will be staying with us." Gary said, as the final word concerning the brief discussion.

Remember me. I'm Pal. I've been listening to Gary's reason for not allowing the girls to have a dog like me in their house. It didn't take long for me to find out the real reason.

Before I tell you what happened, I've been wondering why it's not Uncle Gary and Aunt Megan, Aunt Christi, and Aunt Becky. Back in Florida, its Aunt Cheryl and Uncle Timmy? I'll have to wait and talk to Dad about it. Those names might be a Deep South tradition?

"Dad," I said, as we walked in the front yard so I could go to the potty. "You have a lady friend you call Mom; doesn't Uncle Gary have a Mom too?"

"Pal, it's like this. He had a wife, just like I do, but they didn't get along very well. Two years ago they decided to not live in the same house any longer. Pal, it is what they call these days, a divorce. Now it is just Uncle Gary and his three girls living in this big house. If you are finished I believe we should go in the house."

"Okay, Dad. I hope you and Mom never stop living in our house."

As they all sat in the dining room talking, Gary got up from his chair and opened the dining room door leading to the back porch, and in stepped the biggest dog that ever existed. Now I believe I understand Gary's reason for no more dogs. The girls already have a monster size dog. Interesting though, his name is Stormy and he never walks into the house further than the large rug just inside the dining room door.

For the record, I've decided to call Gary, Uncle Gary; it sounds more proper.

Uncle Gary again picked me up and slowly walked me toward the monster dog he called, Stormy. I was shaking and squirming, but Uncle Gary held me tightly. Holding me he got down on his knees. He held me over to touch and sniff Stormy's nose.

Stormy's reaction was, "*Okay, Gary, put the little kid down; I won't hurt him.*" Shortly, Uncle Gary placed me on the floor beside Stormy's big feet. One of Stormy's paws was almost the size of my whole body. Stormy, just kind of scratched at the floor with his huge feet while making really deep wolfing sounds.

"*Hey, Stormy,*" I said. Stormy and I are communicating, you know! "*Could I ride on your back around the house? That would be fun for me.*"

In his deep echoing voice that only I could hear, Stormy said, "*No, Pal, I'm not allowed in the house. Tomorrow you could come out in the backyard and we can play like that.*"

"*Sure, Stormy, if my Dad takes me outside tomorrow, we will play, but you do know I have to stay in the yard.*"

"*That's not a problem, Pal; my Dad has a big fence all around my backyard. I have to go outside for the night now.*

I see my Dad is putting my supper outside. See you tomorrow, Pal."

Uncle Gary had a huge bag of food for Stormy and he placed some of it outside the door in a giant metal food dish. When Uncle Gary returned, he commented to Mom and Dad. "See, it looks like the two of them will be fine. In the morning I'll take Pal and Stormy along for my morning walk around the neighborhood. Dad, you could come along if you want."

"Good, Gary, I have Pal's leash in the car. Besides, I could use the exercise."

The week went along without any problems. Yes, I did get into a few things I shouldn't. And, yes, one day I couldn't get outside to go, but all things considered, I was on my best behavior. The girls entertained me in their rooms. Stormy was disappointed I never got to ride on his back. Dad had no way of knowing what Stormy and I had talked about earlier.

Apparently Uncle Gary had taken the week off work. Every morning he and Dad would take Stormy and me for long walks. Stormy just walked leisurely along, but I had to almost run to keep up. Shih Tzu's have such short legs, and Stormy, whatever kind of dog he is, has long legs. It sure did tire me out, and when we returned to the house, all I wanted to do was lay down and nap.

It was kind of sad to leave Stormy. The week went by fast and it was time for us to leave. As Dad opened the door of the car for me to jump in, I heard Stormy call from inside the fence, "*Hey, Pal, you come back and see me again sometime soon. Okay?*"

"I would like to do that, Stormy. Bye for now, you be a good dog until I get back. Okay?"

The week ended the way it started when we arrived. After a lot of hugging and kissing, we were off, returning to our good old home in Florida.

CHAPTER 8

Home Improvement Store Visit

Mom kept asking Dad if he could build a front porch. She said she liked to watch the cars go up and down the street. Actually there are only about eight or ten cars a day that do that, but Mom wanted a porch and a chair to sit on it, nevertheless.

Dad talked to Tom, his neighbor that lives across the street about it, and they decided to build the porch. Dad said if we were going to build a porch he wanted an enclosed porch with windows instead of it being open with just screens. A screened porch would allow the summer stormy rains to get the porch wet.

It became an expensive project, but when it was finished, Tom and Dad had insulated it, placed curtains above the five windows, and put a TV in it. They put indoor/outdoor carpet on the floor. Dad and Tom even put in a French door, leading from the porch to the living room where the house picture window had been. For a dog like me, this would be a great new place for me to hang out; I loved it. Dad even moved a recliner to the porch for Mom. Now Mom sits on the porch watching the cars and TV, and I sit in her lap looking out the window, watching for our neighbor across the street. Mom and I both enjoy our new front porch.

One warm day in the spring, Dad wanted to get something from Lowe's Home Improvement Center. Usually, if it is too warm for me to stay in the car while he goes to the store, I have to stay home. This day, however, it was a little on the warm side, but good ole Dad took me along anyhow. When we got to the store, he thought it better not to leave me in the car. Instead he said to me, "I wonder if the store would allow me to quietly sneak you in it in a shopping cart." I was all for it; it was something new. So in the cart I went, sitting in the big part of the basket, lying low so nobody would notice me. At least that's what Dad thought.

We entered the store through the garden center section where there were only one or two people working this particular night. Nobody said a thing to Dad about me, so he went straight into the main section of the store. Dad began looking on the shelves for whatever he wanted, when suddenly there was an announcement over the store's public address system.

"Pets are not permitted at anytime in this store. It is against the law to bring pets in a store that serves food."

Dad's response to the announcement was, "You have to be kidding, Pal. I wonder where the food section is in this home improvement store? It must be something new they're using to try to lure customers into their new store. Hmm! …

They must be providing a restaurant to serve the hungry do-it-yourself home improvement shoppers. What a novel idea. Well, Pal, I didn't want to buy anything here anyhow; let's go before they sic the pet security cops on us." We left through the garden center the same way we came in.

Another time Mom and Dad were going to the grocery store. It was hot outside, so Dad had to leave me home alone. Each time they left me alone, I would get on the 'forbidden' sofa as soon as they left the house. Why I do this, I don't know, but I push all the pillows on the floor. I can't help myself; I just have to do that.

This time, when Dad got in the car, he realized he had forgotten his wallet. He thought he could sneak back in the house through the back door. To do that he had to climb over the four foot wall he had placed between the house wall and the shed. Dad was confident I could never escape my run area in the back yard by jumping his newly installed high wooden wall.

I heard him trying to sneak around back and enter the house through the back door. Just as he was about to put his leg over the fence wall, I jumped it and cleared his little wooden fence, never touching it. "Hooray for me; I was out. Ha! ... And Dad thought he could fence me in my new backyard run area."

An astonished Dad exclaimed, "Wow, Mom, did you see that? Pal never touched the fence. I think we should enter him in some kind of high jump competition. A dog his size shouldn't be able to jump that high."

Seeing what just happened, Mom opened the car door to rescue me, and I immediately jumped into the car with Mom.

"No, Pal, you still can't go along to the store." Having said that, Dad grabbed me from Mom's lap and Dad and I went back in the house. Dad got his wallet and I got a scolding for escaping.

Back in the car Dad said to Mom, "Tomorrow the fenced area gets raised to five feet, and the wall he jumped over gets closed in completely. I'll use our old house front door we took off when Tom and I built the front porch."

Sure enough, the next day Dad and Tom rescued some left over lumber and siding from the front porch project. They began building the wall with a door to the back yard. I wasn't too thrilled about the sawing stuff, but I tolerated it because there were lots of neat things lying around in my backyard run area for me to get into. Concerned for my safety, Dad said, "Pal, you need to go in the house; you're going to get hurt walking around in this stuff."

Tom, defending me, said, "Oh, Dad, he's just like a little kid. He's just curious; he's okay." I like Tom; he's my kind of guy.

The job was completed in just a few hours. When done, Dad said, "Well, Pal, you're looking at the only house in the neighborhood with a door to get into the backyard." Dad was a happy camper, but his part of the fence job wasn't yet complete.

The next morning I heard Dad pounding five foot fence stakes into the ground around my run area. When I came out to see what he was doing, he looked at me and said, "Now, Pal, I'm going to add another two feet to the already three foot fence. I know for sure you won't be able to jump over a five foot fence."

Looking at the height of the five foot poles, I said, "I

think you might be right, Dad. Dad, do you remember the old cowboy song, 'Don't Fence Me In?' I guess I won't sing that anymore because you have definitely fenced me in. My freedom is gone forever."

"I'm just trying to protect you, Pal. Remember the critters we talked about a long time ago."

"Yes."

"Now they won't even try coming over the fence; it's too high for them also."

"Thanks for doing all the good stuff you do for me, Dad."

CHAPTER 9

. . . .

I Visit Cookie's Neighborhood

It has been a long time since we visited Aunt Cheryl's house. Dad didn't need a reason to go, but this time there was a reason; only I don't remember what it was. I just knew I liked to visit her because she has all kinds of neat places to explore; and Aunt Cheryl has a dog too. Her dog was one of those long haired ones she called a mixed breed. I don't understand that, but she called it a cockapoo, I think. All I know is that her dog is a girl and we got along just fine: No sniffing my rear and all that dumb stuff.

The drive to Aunt Cheryl's is not complicated. Follow Interstate 4 northeast for about sixty miles and get off at the correct exit. Realizing we were nearing Cheryl's house, I heard Dad say, "Darn, Mom, I think I just missed the exit to Cheryl's house again."

Mom made her usual comment, "You do that every time.

I would think by now you would know where to get off the interstate."

"Well, Mom, I do know, but with all the construction on the road, it has made the exit look different. I will turn around at the next exit and go back. It's not a problem."

Finally arriving at Aunt Cheryl's, I'm the first out of the car. I can't reach the doorbell, but Aunt Cheryl hears me scratching at the door and opens it.

"Hi, Pal," Aunt Cheryl says, "I was expecting you. Come on in." We all went inside and there was my friend Cookie, the girl dog I was telling you about. We sniffed noses a bit and began running around the house.

"Hey, Cookie," I said. "I have to go out back for a minute. How do we get outside? You don't have one of those little doggie doors like I have at home."

Cookie, in her girlie way said, "Come, follow me, Pal." With that we went into Aunt Cheryl's big backyard. "Anyplace is okay, if you have to go."

Aunt Cheryl has a really high wooden fence all around her entire back yard. I heard her say she had to have it because of her swimming pool. It was a safety thing, I guess. Cookie and I played in the large yard for a while. Finally tired from playing, we decided to go back inside. Aunt Cheryl left the door to the den open a little so we could get in without needing to bark our way back inside.

It wasn't long until I heard Aunt Cheryl tell Timmy, her youngest boy, that everyone was going to the store for something.

Timmy is Dad's grandson. I heard Dad say one time he was fourteen years old. I guess for a kid that is old, but I still like him. He always plays with me. Some people just want to touch me and that's it, but not Uncle Timmy; we play catch and all kinds of neat stuff. He even showed me his pet rabbit that was always hiding in his cage when I come to visit Aunt Cheryl's house. Today Uncle Timmy took the big black rabbit out of the cage and let me smell the strange little critter. He always stays curled up on Uncle Timmy's lap. I don't think the big black ball of fur likes me. "Oh well, that's okay. I'm not too thrilled with him either."

A little later, Uncle Timmy got a ball and took Cookie and me outside in the back yard. Timmy likes to throw the ball and tell us to 'go fetch.' Turns out Timmy did most of the fetching. That was fun for a while until Timmy got tired of fetching our ball. After a bit, Uncle Timmy decided he had enough and went back inside the house, leaving Cookie and me outside alone.

We explored all along the fence when suddenly Cookie disappeared. "Cookie," I called, "where are you?"

From outside the tall fence I heard Cookie say, "I'm out here, Pal, just crawl through that little hole under the fence and we will run around the neighborhood together."

"Cookie, I don't think I should! Dad doesn't allow me to run around our neighborhood alone."

"Nonsense, Pal, besides your Dad isn't here and we will come back inside in just a few minutes."

With a little struggle I managed to wiggle my way through the little hole under the fence. Once outside I looked around and although we were still in Aunt Cheryl's yard, it didn't look familiar. "Come on, Pal," beckoned Cookie. "Let's run up the street and visit with some of the neighbors."

"Okay, if you promise to get me back to Aunt Cheryl's house. You know I don't know this area at all."

Reassuringly Cookie said, "I know every inch of this

place; my Mom lets me run loose all the time! Now, come on; I'll show you around the town; then we will go back in our yard."

I followed Cookie up one street then down another. By one of the houses a little girl was playing in her driveway. The girl called to me and I went up to visit with her. She was nice and I stayed with her to play for a few minutes. In just a short time the little girl's mother called for her to come in her house. Apparently it was her lunch time. After she left me, I was all alone on the sidewalk. Where was Cookie? I didn't see her anyplace.

I've never been left alone like this before. Dad or Mom are always someplace near me. I wanted to call to my Mom or Dad, but I knew they went with Aunt Cheryl. Where was Uncle Timmy? He would take me back to his house, but I didn't see him *or* Aunt Cheryl's house. I'm really lost now. Right then I promised myself I would never go away with Cookie again. I've really been a bad boy this time. "I sure hope Dad can find me when he gets back from the store." I said.

Dad had told me a long time ago, if I ever get lost I should stay in one place, and not run around. Especially, don't go in the street because the cars and trucks could run over me. That's a very scary thought. As those thoughts were going through my head, I decided to ignore Dad's warning words and walk slowly down the street, but staying on the sidewalk. It was no use though; I was lost and I knew it. Not knowing what to do, I went up by a fence at somebody's house, and laid down to rest, and just wait for Dad to find me.

Aunt Cheryl, Mom and Dad arrived home and found

a very excited Uncle Timmy. "Mom," Timmy cried. "Pal is gone. He and Cookie were playing in the back yard! Now they are both gone!"

The panicked bunch quickly went to the back yard to see how the two dogs could have escaped. Aunt Cheryl was first to see the little hole under the fence.

"I never knew there was a hole like that under the fence. Come on, Timmy, we will drive around the neighborhood. We have to find Pal."

Dad and Mom stayed at the house in case I found my way back home; and Timmy and Cheryl began driving around the neighborhood.

Timmy was first to see his longtime friend, Eric and two other boys standing on the sidewalk. "Stop, Mom; I'll ask Eric if he has seen Pal."

"Hey, Eric," Timmy called, "Have any of you seen Pal?"

A nervous Eric said, "Yes, Tim, he's up there by that house." Eric pointed to the house where I had used the fence wall to protect myself from the unfamiliar boys on the sidewalk. "He's over there by the fence, but when we tried to get him, he growled and snapped at us. We were afraid to pick him up because he looked like he was going to bite us."

A very relieved Cheryl said, "You boys stay here on the sidewalk. I'll get him." And with that Cheryl walked slowly up to me. I stood up slowly with my tail wagging as though surrendering to a beautiful friend. "Come on, Pal, let's go home." She picked me up and carried me to her car.

It turns out I had wandered onto a street about three blocks from Aunt Cheryl's house.

I couldn't stop licking Aunt Cheryl. She had rescued me from those awful boys and was taking me to see my Mom and Dad. I said to Cheryl, wishing she could hear, "*I love you, Aunt Cheryl, and I promise I'll never follow another dog, especially a lady dog, anyplace as long as I live!"*

Back at the house I have never been loved by so many or so much. With tears in his eyes Uncle Timmy told his mother he was sorry for failing to watch the two of us. Aunt Cheryl told Timmy they could have escaped, no matter who was keeping them; but she wanted him to fix the hole under the fence with rocks so it couldn't happen again. Uncle Timmy immediately went out and began repairing the hole under the fence.

Mom and Dad loved me a whole lot too. Dad wanted to punish me, but said, "You, being lost in unfamiliar territory, is punishment enough for now." He hugged me and handed me to Mom who wouldn't let me go. That's my mom. She is so good to me, even though I did eat her Hershey candy bar a while back.

As we all sat in the living room, talking about the episode, there was scratching sound at the front door. It was Cookie. Aunt Cheryl opened the front door for her to come inside. Cookie looked at me and said, "Where did you get to, Pal? I looked all over, but I couldn't find you."

My one word response was, "…**You!**"

CHAPTER 10

. . . .

Hello, Mister Bunny Rabbit!

"Ah" I said, "The fresh warm air of spring is finally here again. I like the weather where I live. Dad says Florida is so much better than the cold winter at Uncle Gary's house in Pennsylvania. To celebrate the warm weather I often go out in my run area and just lay on my back in the grass, stretch my legs open, close my eyes, and take a long snooze. You can't beat snoozing in the Florida sunshine."

The back door opened and Dad called, "Come in, Pal; we're going to Aunt Cheryl's house." He never had to tell me more than once that we were going for a ride in the car. It doesn't matter where we go; I'm always ready for a ride in the car.

Today I did hear him talking to Mom about Aunt Cheryl having a birthday. "Another birthday party... Oh, boy ... ice cream and cake. I can't get enough of that."

Unfortunately there was no party stuff when we arrived at Aunt Cheryl's house. Dad informed me that they were all going out to a restaurant to celebrate Aunt Cheryl's birthday, but without me. "Pal, you be good while Aunt Cheryl and the boys are with Mom and me. We should be back in a little while." When Dad says a little while, it could be a few minutes or all night. He never did explain the term *little while*. When someone takes me outside to do my thing before they leave, I have learned I'll be in the house alone for hours.

"Pal," Dad said before leaving, "when we come back from the restaurant, I'll give you a little cake and ice cream. Okay? You be a good boy and don't get into things, do you hear?"

Cheryl was standing in the doorway waiting for her Dad and said, "Okay, Dad, I'm sure he will follow your instructions; now let's go." There is not much left to say about Aunt Cheryl's sarcasm.

Before they left the house I was outside alone with Dad and I asked him, "Dad, where is Cookie?" Dad paused for a moment, then said, "Aunt Cheryl told me Cookie went running in the neighborhood several weeks ago and never came home. She doesn't know if someone stole her or if she was hit by a car. They looked for days, but never found a trace of what happened to her."

"How sad," I thought.

Here I am now, all alone in the Aunt Cheryl's house. At least they left a light on in the house, which was nice of them. Honestly, we dogs don't need light to see in the dark; we just sniff our way around. But Dad remembers my earlier years when I appeared to be afraid in the dark. Always when Dad goes away there is a small light burning and a radio playing.

"I guess Dad thinks I can dance and sing to the music, but unfortunately there is nobody around to dance with me."

"When Aunt Cheryl's house is empty, it sure is quiet. It's kind of spooky, you know?" Suddenly I heard a clanking, jingling noise coming from the dining room. My heart jumped into my mouth and I could feel it beating loud and hard. "Who is it? I can hear you." I said. The sound stopped for a minute, but shortly began again. This time it was clang, clang, jingle, jingle, scratch, scratch. Extremely curious, I began to investigate and found the source. "Oh, it's you." I forgot Uncle Timmy's big black rabbit was in his cage and was looking for a way out. Unfortunately his cage has a gate and has to be opened by Aunt Cheryl or Uncle Timmy to allow him to get out. Apparently when Aunt Cheryl leaves the house the rabbit is locked in his cage. "Too bad, Mister Bunny Rabbit, but I can't open the cage door."

Back at my house Dad keeps everything up high and away from me. At Aunt Cheryl's house there is lots of stuff in the kitchen down low so they keep the rabbit locked inside the cage, just in case.

For the fun of it I said, "If you can get out, come on out, Mister Bunny. I won't hurt you." I know I shouldn't tease the poor thing like that. As I teased him, the rabbit curled into a big black ball at the back of his cage. He apparently was as frightened as I would have been had Mister Bunny suddenly appeared and started staring at me from outside my cage, if I had one.

I decided to go back to the sofa and take a nap. Clearly the rabbit wanted nothing to do with me. Nearly an hour went by when I was suddenly awakened by that sound again. It didn't frighten me this time, because I knew what it was.

Falling asleep again I heard a tiny voice talking, "Hey, mister," the voice of Mister Bunny said. "You promise you won't hurt me?"

I opened one eye and could see Mister Bunny standing up, leaning on the sofa with both front legs next to my face. "Whoa, hey! … Ah … tell me it's you, Mister Bunny!"

"Well, who did you think it was, Mister Pal? You think you are the only one that talks?"

Startled I said, "Not really. I know other animals talk, but when I last saw you, you were curled up in a ball in the back of the cage and the cage door was closed."

The conversation went on with the rabbit saying, "Before I came here to live I worked as a magician's helper. Sometimes he used me in his disappearing hat trick. He had a special cage made for me and I had to magically escape from it during each performance. With considerable effort I eventually learned how to open the door and escape appearing again inside the magician's magical hat. One day the magician realized he was getting much too old to continue his magician act so he sold me, and here I am."

"You are one lucky rabbit to find a nice place like this to live. My name is Pal; what's yours?"

The rabbit had to think for a minute. "I'm not sure. Sometimes the lady calls me Mister and the boy calls me Mister Bunny. Either name is okay with me, as long as they give me food and water. I already know your name is Pal. I've heard them call you that every time you come to visit."

"Hey, Pal," Mister Bunny said, "Let's go in the kitchen and raid the cereal boxes in the cupboard. That's lots of fun. I don't eat it when it spills on the floor, but it's great to hear Cheryl yell at the boys for not cleaning up the spill she thinks they made on the floor."

"You are a trouble maker," I said. "But that does sound like something to do while we are waiting until Mom, Dad, Aunt Cheryl, and the boys get back."

We both went to the kitchen and with very little effort managed to get two boxes of cereal to fall on the floor. Mister Bunny opened the flap on one box and spread a small amount on the floor. I opened another and spilled some. Curious what it tasted like, I began eating. "Hey, Mister Bunny, this Frosty Flake stuff is really good; you ought to try some."

Both of us ate until we were full. Suddenly my ears perked up as I heard the car in the driveway. "Quick, in the cage, Mister Bunny; they're coming home." Mister Bunny ran to the cage and as he entered I could hear the cage door close. I jumped on the sofa and pretended to be sleeping.

"That's odd," Dad said to Mom as they entered the living room. "Pal usually meets us at the door, spinning as he jumps and wags his long tail."

I realized I should look happy to see them, so I jumped up from the sofa and provided Mom and Dad with the expected greeting. Meanwhile Cheryl began giving the boys the dickens for spilling the cereal on the kitchen floor again.

Everyone knows dogs and rabbits can't laugh, but I was standing beside the rabbit cage, looking at Mister Bunny, wanting to do a tee-hee. Instead, I placed my right paw high on the outside of the cage. Mister Bunny did the same from inside as we both did a high five.

CHAPTER 11

My Friend Across the Street

In the spring Dad gets the noisy gas powered shrub trimmer out and trims all the bushes in the yard. He says spring is the time to give the shrubs a fresh new haircut. "It makes them bloom better in early spring and summer." Mom thinks Dad cuts all of her beautiful shrubs back much too far. *Mutilates*, is what Mom says he does to them.

Usually Dad ties me to a pole when he works in the yard, but this day he allowed me to stay unleashed with him in the backyard as he worked. Suddenly, in the corner of my eye I spotted a big black stray cat in our yard. In a mighty dash I chased after the cat. Going berserk, the cat dashed for the next door neighbor's yard as its way of escape. As a stray, one would think the cat would know there is a wire fence between our yard and the next door neighbor's yard. As the cat ran at top speed, suddenly he slammed against the neighbor's fence, stopping him in his tracks. Not knowing where to run, he stopped and hunched his back up, screaming and hissing at me. He looked like one of those scary Halloween cat pictures. I, on the other hand, stopped considerably back from the yelling thing. Dad was hollering at me to come back, and when I turned to look at him, the cat ran full speed out of our yard and across the street to Dad's friend's house, Tom and Jamie. Of course, I did the same and Dad ran as fast as he could after me. I never thought Dad could run that fast.

He caught me and gave me a smack on the backside, saying, "Pal, you better hope you never catch that cat. If you do, it will cut you open with its long sharp claws. Then what would I do? … I'd have to take you to Dr. Robinson and hope she could fix the cuts and scratches you got from your cat encounter."

"But, Dad, all I want to do is play."

"No buts, Pal, you don't play with stray cats. Besides they could have all kinds of diseases, and I'm sure they have fleas. You don't play with the stray cats that come in our yard. ***Do you understand?***"

"Yes, Dad."

Tom was working on his car in his driveway and Jamie, his wife, was sitting in a chair watching him when she heard the commotion. When Dad was finished scolding me, Jamie said, "Come here, Pal, to Aunt Jamie. I'll hold you close and your mean old Daddy won't paddle you anymore."

Dad dropped me to the ground and I ran to Aunt Jamie, who immediately picked me up and snuggled me close. I really like Jamie and Tom.

When Dad goes out our front door, I try to go with him.

I'm not always successful, but when I am, I look over to see if Tom or Jamie are outside. If they are, I immediately run across the street to see them. Dad yells at me to stop, but usually I don't. That makes Dad angry. The reason he gets angry is because he is afraid a car will hit me. I never look to see if there is traffic coming. There is not much traffic on our street, but Dad says it only takes one time to be hit and that would be the end of me.

Jamie and Tom have two small dogs named Killer and Harley. When the two of them are out, they both chase me all over their yard. The problem is, both of them like to sniff me and jump all over me. I guess they think I'm a lady dog, but we know I'm not. At least I think I'm not. When they get too sniffy and jumpy, Tom or Jamie pick me up to protect me. I don't know why dogs do that kind of stuff and Dad has never explained it to me.

About every two weeks Dad invites me into his bathroom. Unfortunately I know what that means, especially when I see my old worn and faded bath towel hanging on his bathroom door. That is a sure sign it's my bath time. It's not all that bad getting a bath, but I just like pretending I don't like it. Dad tries to lure me in by saying I am looking scruffy and starting to smell really bad. I don't know about your children, but most kids would say, "Who cares?" As a dog, I think pretty much along that same bit of logic. Dad takes it one step further, however, and will say, "A bath will make you smell really good." Those words get me every time. If you remember, I sometimes sleep on his pillow at night. Enough said.

When I notice his bathtub shower curtain is on the outside of the tub, I know for sure I'm going for a swim in his bathtub. After the first soap is squirted on me, Dad scrubs me with a brush, and then rinses the soap off with his hand held shower head. The part I really don't like is the soap and rinse water on my face. He tells me the soap is the special Oatmeal kind that doesn't burn the eyes. "I don't know how he would know what kind of shampoo burns the eyes of a dog." The soap is not the problem, however. The problem is the rinsing me off with water. Sometimes the water from the sprayer goes up my nose. When that happens, I sniff and cough and shake my head, splashing water all over him. That's the only fun I get when he gives me a bath. Splashing Dad is fun.

Then Dad gives me a second bath. Dad says the second bath is to keep the fleas off me. I had fleas one time and I'm glad this kind of soap keeps me flea free. That one time the fleas nearly caused me to scratch all the fur off my body. Nasty critters, those fleas are.

If there is a good part to all this bath stuff, it is the blow drying part. Dad takes me in his bedroom and convinces me to hop on his bed. I willing do that because I know he is going to use the little hair dryer, with its warm air, to dry my furry body. It feels so good to have him comb my hair, especially on my belly. When he is finished he gives me a hug and says, "Now you can sleep on my pillow again. You look good and smell really great. For being such a good boy today you deserve a treat." That's the best part of the whole routine.

Speaking of fleas, I became infested with ticks a long time ago. In fact they were so bad that Dad had to take me to see the veterinarian. Dr. Robinson showed him how to pick the ticks off my body using tweezers. He also got a lesson on how ticks can get in the house and what to do about them. Before we left the clinic the doctor asked Dad if I had been in the woods. He told her no, but Pal does lie outside at times in his run area. She asked him if there is any of the ground cover in the run area covered in pine bark nuggets. Dad said only in the flower areas.

"That's where the ticks are coming from. Ticks lay their eggs in the notches of the pine bark and from there they get on the dog. Actually," she said, "when the tick hatches, they climb on the bushes, and when the dog walks under the bush, the tick drops down onto the back of the dog, much like a spider would." She said "Ticks are related to the spider family, you know."

Next day Dad spent most of the afternoon raking the pine nuggets out of my fenced run area. To make sure he got the critters under control he sprayed insecticide over the entire part of my run area. Later he tied me outside and explained that he was going to spray insecticide throughout the entire house. He didn't want me breathing the spray stuff. I suppose it's not a good thing to smell the insecticide.

As he was spraying in the house, he said he noticed a tiny tick climbing up a curtain in his bedroom. That reinforced what the doctor told him about ticks climbing things.

Thunder and lightening in the summertime scare me. I talk often to Dad and wonder why it frightens me so much. I can hear the boomers when they are far from the house. If I'm near the window and I see a distant flash of light in the sky, I run to Mom or Dad to hide. I know the boom is coming soon, so I jump up on Mom's lap and hide my head. I can't help it; I shake and shiver all over. Mom always says to me, "Pal, don't be afraid; you are safe in the house with me." But that is no comfort.

On the Fourth of July and New Years Day people around the neighborhood set off fireworks and that frightens me too. I heard Dad talking to Tom one time. Dad said he wondered if the boom sounds of a fireworks show he took Mom and I to when I was a tiny baby could be the reason for my fright. Tom said it probably was. He said Pal might get over it, but his two dogs, Killer and Harley are the same way. "A little thunder in the area and Harley and Killer go nuts." I don't know what that means, but if it means they get scared like me, it must be a dog thing.

CHAPTER 12

. . . .

Mom Needs My Help

It was a really warm mid July evening. I decided to lay on the porch. There is a large plastic container under the open window that had a big comfortable pillow on top of it. Dad placed it under the window so I could see the exciting activities happening outside. It is much cooler lying on the new front porch, rather than on Mom's lap. I love her, but I can only take so much body heat, and her lap does get very warm.

Mom said she was going to bed, which was rather early for her, I thought. I can't tell time yet, but I did hear the mantle clock strike ten just before the TV went off. I suppose you're surprised to know I can count; sometime, perhaps I'll tell you how I learned. Mom usually wakes up when the Tonight Show is over and that's around twelve-thirty. That's the time she *usually* goes to bed.

Shortly after the TV went off, I heard a loud boom coming from the living room. Mom made a loud crying sound as she fell to the floor. I jumped up and went to see what had happened and found her lying on the floor, crying, "Pal, *Pal*, I can't get up! I think my leg is broken! … What am I going to do, Pal? Dad won't be home from work until at least three in the morning! … I can't move, Pal!"

I wanted to tell Mom to just lay still and maybe I could bark loud enough for Tom or Jamie to hear and come over and help her. That's all I can do, and I did. I barked until my barker nearly quit, but it was no use. If only I could use the telephone, but I can't reach it. It was no use. All I could do is lay my head on Mom's arm and wait. Mom didn't try to move because the few times she tried it, she screamed in pain. I lay on her arm for hours. The clock struck three in the morning so I knew Dad would be home soon. Finally, I heard the sound of his car in the driveway. I got up and ran to the door, barking for him to come quickly.

As Dad was coming in the front door I could hear him say, "Pal, what's wrong? You and Mom should be in bed."

"Come quick, Dad; Mom fell down."

Dad hurried into the living room and found Mom on the floor, "Oh, honey, don't try to move. When did you fall?" He asked her as he was dialing 911.

Mom tried to remember, but she had no idea what time she fell. "I don't know when I fell. I was just getting up and here I am. I'm so sorry to cause you so much trouble, honey. Pal stayed right here with me, lying on my arm the whole time. He's such a good Pal."

Dad said, "The ambulance will be here in just a few minutes, honey; just lay still; don't try to move!"

This is something new and awful to me and I don't know what to expect. In just a few minutes I heard a big truck noise outside on the street and saw bright flashing red lights. Dad said it was the ambulance, "*I wonder what will happen now?*" I thought.

Two men came rushing to the door and stopped before opening it. What are they going to do? I managed to bark again and that is what stopped them from opening the front door. Dad heard the commotion and told me to get back, "Pal, they're here to help your Mommy; now stop growling and let the men come in." Dad opened the door and one of them held his hand down for me to sniff. They seemed friendly enough and smelled okay, so I let them in the house.

I guess the men are okay, but the quick motions of the men bending over Mom scared me. I didn't want them to hurt my Mommy. Soon, two more men came in the door. They asked Mom some questions, but she couldn't give them any answers about what happened.

One of the men went outside to his big truck and came back with a bed like thing on wheels. One of the men that was in charge said, "On the count of three. One … two … three." When he said "three" the men lifted Mom gently onto the bed thing. Mom made a loud groan, and immediately the ambulance men rolled Mom outside, placing her inside the big ambulance truck. Before they left the house, one of the men told Dad they would take Mom to Heart of Florida Hospital. Before leaving the man said to Dad, "They'll fix her up good as new."

Dad went to the hospital every day for several weeks, sometimes two times a day. He tried to explain to me that Mom couldn't come home until she was healed. "Pal, the doctors won't fix the leg until her heart gets better." I don't know what Dad meant, except Mom didn't come home.

One day Dad came home and said the doctors decided Mom's heart seemed better so they operated on her hip and fixed her broken leg. The doctor told Dad she would have to go to a nursing home first before coming home. Dad explained, "The nursing home will give her exercises to help her walk again. I might be allowed to take you there to see her. Would you like that, Pal?"

"I sure would like to see my Mommy again. I miss her so much."

Every day Dad would take me to the nursing home to see Mom. Each time, before we went into the nursing home to visit Mom, Dad would stop me and say, "Pal, you have to go to the potty outside. We don't want any potty mess in her room. Okay?"

Understanding, I said, "I can do that."

It didn't take me long to sniff my way to Mom's room. Sometimes I would visit other people before going to see Mom. All the people liked to play with me, but I didn't stay with them long because I knew Mom was waiting anxiously to see me.

For a while Mom had her meals in bed, but then one day the nurses placed her in a chair that had wheels on it. I would ride along on the chair with her to the dining room on her lap. After a few times of doing that, the head nurse told Dad, "Pets are not permitted in the dining room during the patient's meal time."

"That's not fair," I said. "What a bummer!"

Dad said Mom was supposed to get physical therapy

every day to help her learn to walk again. She did it for about a week or so, but then she began to refuse the help of the therapy nurse; instead she stayed in her bed. Dad told me Mom had given up hope of ever getting better.

Even so, Dad kept going to the nursing home, taking me along nearly every time. The last few times I went to visit Mom, she didn't even know who I was. She didn't even know Dad. That made Dad very sad.

Dad was beginning to fix himself breakfast at the house when the telephone rang. Dad raced to answer it. It was the nursing home Hospice nurse calling. When he hung up he began to cry. "Pal, it's all over. We won't be going to the nursing home anymore! ... The nurse said Mom gave up living a few minutes ago." The time was 8:30 am, August 24, 2005.

"It would be nice if someone could stay with me at night after Dad goes to work, but they don't. I sure do miss my Mommy."

CHAPTER 13

. . . .

All Dad Wanted Was Coffee

Aunt Cheryl and Uncle Timmy often come to our house for visits. Aunt Cheryl suggested one time that we all go to the nearby small town named Celebration. Dad said it is one of those areas that has a downtown area with shops and restaurants, and even sidewalks. That might sound strange to mention *sidewalks* as a feature, but in our part of Florida there are very few sidewalks. In fact, where we live there are no sidewalks and you must always walk in the street. Going to Celebration sounded exciting. I am always ready to visit new places. Being able to walk around the neighborhood without fear of being run over by a car is definitely a plus; I don't care where it is.

It is a short drive to Celebration from our house. As we drove into the town, immediately I saw it was full of big pretty houses and beautiful lawns. It looked kind of like where Uncle Gary lives. The houses are not small things like where I live; instead they are big, two and three story ones. "Someday," Dad said, "it would be nice to live here." Then he added, "But I'm too old to even think about that." He continued to drive up and down the street, enjoying the beauty of it all and commenting about the pretty flowers in the yards.

Dad parked the car by the lake in the downtown area, put me on my leash, and we began walking. This is a new adventure for me, for sure. It seemed like everyone had their dog out for a walk on this day. Young people, old people, even children strolling around the lake were being led around by their leashed dogs. That's the law, you know, especially in this town: no pets are allowed to run loose. What a beautiful place; life is good.

We walked on the sidewalks by the downtown area stores, doing what Aunt Cheryl called window shopping. Apparently Dad and Aunt Cheryl didn't need to buy anything because we didn't even go into one of the stores. There is this one place that had chairs and tables on the sidewalk. Dad said it is an outside restaurant. What a novel idea! I like it. I know I'm never allowed to go inside a restaurant or a store, what with all the health rule stuff. Some people think of us as animals and we could be a serious health risk. "I know I'm not a dirty animal, but Dad said I still can't go in the stores! — That's a bummer again."

The outside restaurant looked inviting so the four of us sat at a little table far away from the other diners. Lest you think I was seated at the table, clear your mind of that picture, I was on the end of my leash, lying under the table.

Dad knows table manner rules: no dogs seated at the table. I hate that, but rules are rules.

We waited for a long time. Dad finally said, using his most annoying loud voice, "Cheryl, I wonder if the waiter is *ever* going to take our evening snack order. Some of these people sat down *after us* and they already have their food."

We waited and waited, and eventually a man appeared in a white shirt and tie, who said he was the manager of the restaurant. "Sir," he was talking to Dad. "I'm sorry, but you will have to leave this area. Pets are not permitted in the serving area, health regulations, you know."

"Well, sir," Dad explained, "in case you haven't noticed we are outside on the sidewalk."

The manager, thinking he would have the last word, said, "I'm sorry, sir, but you must leave now."

Dad cannot quit; he has to be the last to speak and so he said, as we slowly got up to leave, "*Sir*, I have been inside your restaurant and frankly *I think* it is much cleaner eating out here, *so there!*" I know that isn't much of a come back, but Dad doesn't always make sense to me either.

"Come on, guys," Dad said, "all I wanted was a cup of coffee anyhow."

Uncle Timmy was the first to notice a Starbuck's across the street. "Timmy," Dad said, "you might find it hard to believe, but I don't think I have ever had Starbuck's coffee. You hold Pal's leash while I go inside and get my coffee."

As Dad entered the coffee shop, he noticed a sign stating, 'Pets Welcome In This Area.' Dad went back to the sidewalk and beckoned Uncle Timmy to bring me into an outside Starbuck's table area. Dad was finally renewing his faith in the human race. By now he had cooled down considerably.

The cool evening was a joy for me to behold. It had been

a new experience for me, seeing so many other kinds of dogs. This is a fun place for us dogs to run around. I hope Dad will bring me here again.

It is amazing how single men, especially old ones, change their eating habits. Now that he's alone, Dad rarely cooks, especially breakfast and lunch. For breakfast he has a bowl of cereal and for lunch some kind of microwave stuff. He says he doesn't want a bunch of cooking utensils to wash and dry after he is finished eating. His washed and clean dish rack consists of a cereal bowl and a small dessert dish that he uses for his ice cream treat at night. He has a large glass and a small juice glass. The juice glass is for his prune juice that he uses to wash down his morning vitamins and his blood pressure pill. Then in the utensil tray is a knife, a small spoon, a fork, a soup spoon, and a large spoon which is used to scoop the ice cream treat in the evening. Dad says he needs the large soup spoon because with his tremor problem in his left hand the food won't stay on the fork. I tell him, "Eat with your right hand if the tremor is a problem."

Dad's comeback is, "Pal, have you noticed, I'm left handed?"

Trying to be helpful, I said, "A lot of people can do things with either hand. Remember, Dad, on TV some baseball players bat left or right handed."

Again Dad has to be last to speak. "I'm not batting, Pal; I'm trying to eat, not play baseball! So forget it!" I never mentioned it again.

For lunch he takes a microwave TV dinner from the freezer, every time reading the directions about how long to microwave it. Since he eats the same thing all the time, one would think he would remember the amount of time it takes to cook the stuff, but he doesn't. Even I could remember that much. When the dinner is cooked, he takes the plastic tray to the table along with a glass of vegetable juice. Dad says eating is a requirement to stay alive; that's the only reason he does it.

Except for our nightly ice cream treat, that is pretty much Dad's food for the day. Occasionally he will place the plastic tray on the floor for me to lick. Sometimes I'll eat the vegetable stuff, but most of the time I just sniff it and walk away. I know Dad does not understand why, but I know some of the stuff he eats is not good for me. The exception is when Dad gives me the empty lasagna tray to lick. I chase that tray all over the house, trying to get every morsel off the sides of the empty tray. When I'm finished licking it clean, Dad could use the tray for something else, but he never does.

CHAPTER 14

. . . .

Amazing What a Dog Can Do

Why do bad things always seem to happen at night? Dad tells me that is not true, but at our house it seems to be.

On this day, Dad had awakened early, just as the sun was coming up. As he stepped out of bed, he immediately fell to the floor, screaming in pain. "What's wrong, Dad? *Get up!*" I screamed at him.

Through his tears of pain, he said, "Pal, my back and my legs… I can't move my legs! … I can hardly move, Pal; go to the living room and with your mouth try to pull on the telephone cord; that will cause the portable phone to fall on the floor. I think I can drag myself to the phone if you can get it to fall on the floor. I need to get some help. Try, Pal; please try to do that for me!"

If I did something like this any other time, Dad would kill me, but he needed my help. I could see the telephone cord running up the wall, but Dad had fastened it to the wall, and I couldn't pull it loose. Running back into the bedroom, I said, "Dad, you fastened the phone cord to the wall and I can't do what you are asking."

"You're right, Pal. Let me think. Pal, … the small sofa love seat is nearly against the wall where the telephone is, you can stand high on the sofa back. Try to reach your paw to the telephone handset and knock it off. It should fall on the floor."

Listening to Dad cry in pain is more than I can stand, so I would do anything to help my Dad. I went back into the living room and I could see the portable telephone in the cradle, high on the counter between the kitchen and the living room. I jumped up on the back of the love seat, trying to reach across to the kitchen counter top, but it was a long stretch. If I can stretch my body across the big space between the sofa and the counter top, I know I can knock it to the floor. "Here goes nothing." I did what Dad said and I stretched my paw, touching the counter top. "**Whoa**! … **Oh, wow! Ouch!** Hey, Dad! … I fell down, but I'll try again! I almost had it!"

"Keep trying, Pal. I know you can do it." Dad said, as he continued crying loudly in pain.

"One more time; that fall didn't hurt me much." I was beginning to talk aloud to myself just like Dad does. I looked and studied the phone cord coming up the wall from the floor and going over the edge of the counter top, "I should be able to reach the cord and pull the whole phone over the edge. That should make the portable phone fall to the floor"

Standing again on the sofa back, I reached for the telephone cord and with my claws I snagged it. As I did, the whole telephone came crashing to the floor, bouncing off my head. I fell to the floor also. "Ouch, ouch! … Oh, man, that really hurt!"

Dad, hearing the noise, called, "You okay, Pal? Did you get it down?"

"***Yes, Dad!*** … Now you stay in the bedroom; don't try to crawl out here! I think I can get the little antenna part of the phone in my mouth."

With considerable difficulty I managed to get the portable phone in my mouth and managed to drag it to Dad in his bedroom.

A relieved Dad said, "Good boy, Pal. Now I'll call Tom across the street, using the speed dial thingy."

In not more than a minute Tom rushed in and analyzed the situation. "Lee, I'm calling 911." Tom said, "You need professional help. You need to go to the hospital."

When Tom said that, chills went through my body. The last time Mom went to the hospital, she never came back. What would I do if Dad never came home again?

The big ambulance truck came again and with extreme difficulty the men took Dad outside to the truck, leaving me alone in the house.

I waited and waited for Dad to come back, but he didn't. Many hours went by before I heard a car pull into the driveway. I raced to the window to see who it was. It was Aunt Cheryl's car. What a welcome sight! Maybe she came to take me to her house. Aunt Cheryl would take me home with her; I know she would.

The other car door opened and I saw Dad holding on to Aunt Cheryl, and they both came in the house. This is a happy day for me: my Dad *did* come home. He looks sick, but at least he came back. I jumped up to Dad as he came in the door.

"Pal, stay down! Don't jump!" Dad said, as he carefully moved into the living room and did a very slow painful sit down in his recliner. "The hospital gave me some shots of medicine, Pal. They said it would not be long before the pain would go away completely, but at least I was allowed to come home."

Aunt Cheryl said, "Dad, you do know Pal is a dog. *Right?* You talk to him like he understands you. *He is just a dog,* Dad."

"Sure, Cheryl, he is a dog, a very special dog. You do know he is the one that brought the telephone to me in my bedroom. That's the only way I could call Tom and get his help. Yes, I know Pal is a dog, but Pal is a very special dog to me."

Dad looked at me and said, "Pal, sometime I'll have to teach you how to dial 911. That could be a life saver for me."

I looked up at Dad, holding up a paw as though saying, "Sure, Dad, but look at my feet. Have you noticed? I don't have fingers? I don't even have a thumb!"

Dad carries a card in his wallet now that says; "In case of emergency call Cheryl." It's a good thing Dad carries that card; otherwise, who would the doctors or the hospital know to call? I thought about that for myself. Maybe I should have some way to identify who I belong to in case I get lost like I did at Aunt Cheryl's place a long time ago. "When Dad gets better, I'll have to talk to him about that."

It took a while for Dad to get back to work, but the

medicine the doctor gave him made him all better. I was happy to have my Dad back playing with me.

Until now, Dad has been working five and six nights a week. After his last sickness episode, he decided it was time to slow down and just work part time: two days a week. Now he is home with me every day except Thursday and Friday night. Dad now works, what he calls, third shift. He leaves the house about seven at night and gets home about seven in the morning. We have lots of time to play together. He tries to pretend he is busy, but I pester him, and he finally concedes and plays with me. What a neat Dad!

If you have been following my story until now, it would appear all I do is get in trouble at home and ride in the car. The fact is; Dad takes me for walks nearly every day, all the way to the mail box. On Saturdays and Sundays we go to the school playground located just down the hill behind our mobile home development. Dad turns me loose without my leash. It is a big open field where the kids play soccer. Dad said the children kick a big ball around, sometimes kicking it in a net located at each end of the field. Sounds like fun for me, but he said I can't be there when the boys and girls are playing. The best I can do with Dad is chase after a big stick he throws. I'm supposed to find it and take it back to him. Sometimes I do, but most of the time I find it and run to the other end of the field and chew on it. It takes Dad a long time to catch up to me. He tries to take it away from me, but I'm pretty fast on my feet, and I guess he is old, and he doesn't run like he did years ago. To trick me, he finds another stick and throws it. If I feel like running, I get the new stick. It is great fun playing with Dad.

Then there is the walk to the mailbox every day. The mail is delivered to a community mailbox located about three blocks from the house. I am pretty obedient most of the time and walk beside Dad like I'm supposed to. One time during our walk I became distracted along the way by something and I simply stopped walking. He kept going, holding onto my now empty leash that had slipped over my head. It didn't take him long to realize that I wasn't on the end of the leash. To say Dad became angry is an understatement. "I'm going to get a harness and put it on you when we walk together. Then we'll see if you can slip out of that! … I think not."

Sure enough, the next day Dad came home from the store with a thing that slips over my head and behind my front legs. He called it a harness. I thought they only made those for horses, but lo and behold, Dad has one for me, a dog. "I'm not going to like this thing; I know it!"

Next day when it was time for the mailbox walk, Dad was trying to figure out how the contraption worked. He had it upside down, inside out, and finally after half an hour figured out how it went on. *"Interesting gadget,"* I thought. *"but I'm not walking with this thing on!"*

"Let's go, Pal; its mailbox time." Dad said.

"That's okay, Dad, you go without me. If I have to wear this silly thing, I'm not going!"

"But, Pal, it's just a thing to keep you from getting hit by a car. When you slip out of the collar, you get away from me, and sometime a car might hit you!"

Using a rather insolent tone, I said, "Oh sure, like a horse collar thingy will keep a car from hitting me."

A determined Dad said, "You will wear it and that is that!

Now, come on!" And with that said he snapped the leash to the harness and dragged me out the door.

"Stop, Dad, this thing is rubbing the back of my front legs." But he didn't stop. I walked a few steps and stopped completely. Dad kept going with me still attached to the harness. It is amazing how many times you can flip in circles while someone holds the leash tight. Dad yelled at me again to stop fooling around and walk. I did for about ten more steps, and again I did acrobatic flips while he tried to walk forward.

Dad said, "You sure can be a stubborn fellow. Okay, Pal, you win! Now, go back to the house and wait there until I get back from the mailbox." I'm not bad like that all the time, and when Dad told me to go home, I went home. Actually, I didn't have to go very far; we were still in front of our house, so I just sat on the front porch steps and waited for him to return from the mailbox. "I showed him who is boss in this family!"

CHAPTER 15

. . . .

My Christmas Baby Sitter

At Christmas 2007, it was what to do, where to go! I really don't like the conversation I'm hearing Aunt Cheryl and Dad talking about on the telephone.

"Cheryl," Dad is saying as he talked on the phone, "I really can't afford to fly to Ohio to see Dennis for Christmas. … But, Cheryl, you have so much expense with Matthew and his Embry Riddle tuition. I do not want you paying my airplane fare to Ohio. … Well, Cheryl, if Gary is going to be there, it would be nice to have a family reunion in Ohio. Our family hasn't been together for years. … Are Matthew and Timmy also going? … They are? … Okay, I'll go, but I don't know if I'll ever be able to pay you back! … Somehow I will, but I don't know when. You had better hope I live 'till I'm at least a hundred."

Now I know the plan. Dad is going to see his oldest son in Xenia, Ohio. He told me it's near Dayton. That doesn't help though. I don't know where that is either. Oh, well. "Hey, Dad," I said with a heavy heart sound in my voice. "How long will you be gone?

"Only a week, Pal."

"You're not putting me in that kennel again, are you?"

"No, Pal." Dad said, trying to sound upbeat. "Do you remember Terri, the lady that stays with Jamie's Killer and Harley when Tom and Jamie go on vacation?"

"Sure I do. She comes to visit me sometimes when Jamie and Tom are away." That is how Dad knows I really like Terri.

"Tomorrow," Dad said. "I'll call Terri and see if she can sit with you here at our house while I'm away."

As promised, Dad called Terri about the Christmas 'dog sitting' job. Terri said she could do it if she could take me to her mother's house on Christmas Day. Terri told Dad some of her family would be getting together like they do every Christmas.

"Pal, I talked to Terri and she is going to be with you every day I'm away. She said she would be taking you to her Mom's house for Christmas dinner. Do you think you could behave at a stranger's house?"

"Me, behave at a stranger's house? I don't know why you would think any different of me, Dad! You don't have to worry about me; I'll be a good boy. They might even allow some turkey to fall on the floor as they eat. Of course I'd have to clean that up, you know!"

Dad gave me one of those skeptical looks and said, "I

don't know about this arrangement, Pal, but I don't have any choice on this one."

The big day came for Dad's airline flight. He had asked Terri to drive him to the airport. When Terri arrived at our house, he loaded his suitcase and me in her car. "Wow, I get to see the big airport. This is going to be great." I sat quietly on the console between the front seats as Dad explained the time for Terri to pick him up when he returns. He offered to give her gas money, but she refused to accept it. Dad also loaned her his toll thing so she could take the E-pass lane, passing quickly through all the toll booths without paying tolls. Dad is good about that kind of stuff.

Dad was making use of his cell phone that Aunt Cheryl had given him. It has taken him a long time to reliably talk to anyone on the cell phone, but this time he had success telling Aunt Cheryl they were near the airport. Dad wanted her to meet him at the airport departure area. Sure enough, when we arrived at the airport, Aunt Cheryl and Uncle Timmy were standing outside waiting for Dad. Aunt Cheryl said Matthew was coming also, but on a later flight. Dad took his suitcase from Terri's car, gave me a hug, and gave Terri a kiss on the cheek. Hmm, … wonder what that's about.

Anyhow, this is to be my first night with Aunt Terri. This should be a vacation for me also.

Aunt Terri was to sleep in the big bed that used to be Mom's. She didn't have trouble with me sleeping on the bed until I laid my head above hers on the pillow. "Pal, you have to sleep at the bottom of the bed."

I began to wonder about Aunt Terri. To myself I said, "*This could be a long night, but I'll go to the bottom of the bed if that's what she wants.*" Before long I could hear Aunt Terri breathing heavy, so I knew she was fast asleep. Softly I tiptoed back to the pillow and took my place above her head. "It's not my fault she doesn't give me enough space above her head. I tried not to breathe in her face, but she was so close to me I couldn't help it. Dad doesn't like me breathing on his face either."

It didn't take long for Aunt Terri to realize that I was back on her pillow. "That's it, Pal; *out you go!*" And with one quick move she picked me up and put me outside the bedroom door, closing it as she went back to bed. "Pal," she said from the bedroom. "unless you can sleep at the bottom of the bed, you will have to stay in the living room alone all night."

It sounded to me like she meant it. Now what? I scratched and scratched on the closed door. I tried pushing it hard, but it wouldn't open. Aunt Terri locked me in the living room all alone. From the bedroom I heard her say, "Pal, you stay alone when your Daddy goes to work; now go to his bedroom and go to sleep." But I was determined to be with Aunt Terri. I continued to scratch on her door. Apparently the scratching noise irritated her and the bedroom door suddenly burst open! She picked me up and tossed me on the bed saying. "*Now, you stay down at the bottom of the bed and we will both sleep fine! Okay?*"

I think I better do as she says. "I don't want her to go home and leave me all alone."

After that run-in with her, Aunt Terri and I got along great. During the day she went to work, but when she came home in the evening she always played with me for a bit and gave me a special treat. I love this lady!

Several times she took me to her house. I did my best not to get into her stuff. After the bedroom incident, I couldn't take any chances. We went for long walks and I never did my stop quick trick where the collar slips over my head. I didn't want to take a chance of her getting out the harness thing. Life is good even though Dad is not here.

Christmas morning we piled into Aunt Terri's car that was filled with lots of pretty decorated packages. She drove the short distance north to her Mom's house. When we arrived at her Mom's house, a bunch of people came out to greet us. Most of them knew I was coming, and they picked me up and hugged me like a long lost relative. I have a feeling this is the beginning of a fun kind of day for me!

How exciting, there are going to be lots of people to play with me. We all went inside the house and gathered around the Christmas tree. There were a lot of pretty packages placed all around it. Aunt Terri said she had a special package for me too. "Wow, something for me among all these things. I can hardly wait."

"Here, Pal," Aunt Terri said, "this one is for you." She wanted me to jump into her lap and I did. She was holding a pretty red and green wrapped package that smelled like some kind of bone. Aunt Terri opened it for me. I could have chewed it open myself, but with all these people looking at me, why should I?

Sure enough, it was a big bone like Dad buys for me sometimes at the Super Center. He bought one of these for me months ago and I chewed on it for days. It has a beef flavor, but I don't think it is beef at all. Whatever it is, it's good and I liked it. I wanted to tell Aunt Terri "Thank you!" but she couldn't hear me, so I just gave her a little kiss on the cheek, just like Dad did at the airport.

Apparently the Christmas dinner was very good. Everyone

ate some, then they ate some more. It amazed me that a few of the people eating, seemed to spill things on the floor. You know, of course, I had to lick up their careless spills. When they finished, they all went into the living room, settled back on the chairs and sofa, and began talking about the old time days at Christmas. I went into the living room also. I found a safe place to roll over on my back, spread my legs, and nap like most of the other folks. It was great!

The week went by quickly. It was time to pick up Dad at the airport. This time Aunt Terri said I had to stay at the house. Seems there was some confusion about the time to pick up Dad, so she thought it best if I stayed behind.

I waited and waited, and finally I heard Aunt Terri's returning car in the driveway. I hurried to the door and did my welcome dance in circles for Dad as he entered the house. It was good to have him home again. Aunt Terri came inside also. Dad thanked her over and over for taking care of me. She told Dad she couldn't stay the night and needed to go home, so he paid her for the week and gave her gas money for her trouble of using her car to pick him up at the airport. Then he gave her a big hug and again, kissed her on the cheek. Dad said he liked her because he could trust her to take good care of me. Boy, did she ever take good care of me.

As we get older, time passes quickly, at least that's what Dad says each year his birthday comes around.

"Pal," Dad said, "It's April 9th. Do you know what day this is?"

"I would know if you gave me a hint, Dad."

Trying to prolong the mystery, Dad said, "Does blowing out candles mean anything to you?

"Only thing I can think of, Dad, is you might be blowing out *your birthday candles;* you must be getting older."

"No, smarty pants!" Dad has a way with words. "It is your birthday. Today it's your turn to get older. Mine was last October. Didn't you see me this morning in the kitchen baking a cake?"

"Well, I saw you using pans you never used before. I did wonder what you were doing."

Dad went into the kitchen and returned with the cake that had a big number five candle on top of it. He picked me up and sat me on a chair at the dining room table, and lit the candle. Then he sang 'Happy Birthday' to me. "Today," Dad said. "you are five years old. In people years you are catching up to me. In dog years, you are nearly thirty-five! Can you believe it?" It was good to hear Dad sing, and it was even better when he gave me a little piece of cake and some vanilla ice cream. No chocolate ice cream though! What a bummer! My Dad is so good to me.

CHAPTER 16

. . . .

Dad Explains a Brain Aneurism

As I explained earlier, Dad works the all night shift part-time on Thursday and Friday. For some reason I heard his car in the driveway and it wasn't even morning. In fact, I heard the mantle clock strike four. Why would he come home so early? It didn't take long to find out why.

As Dad came in the house, the telephone was ringing and he hurried to answer it.

Aunt Christi was calling from her home in Pennsylvania. Dad was quiet, and as he talked, he said, "If the doctors say he won't come out of the coma, Christi, and more than one doctor agrees with that decision, I would have to say, pull the plug." ... Dad paused as he listened to Christi talk. ... "I know, Christi; he's my son, but he is *your* Dad. You must do what you and your sisters think is best. ... Personally I would have the doctors pull the plug. Having him become a vegetable is not what Gary would want for the three of you; I am sure of that!" … The telephone conversation went on for a few more minutes. … "Thank you so much for calling me, Christi. Cheryl and I will be in touch later after the three of you make your decision. … Christi, it sounds to me like God has already made the decision for you."

When Dad hung up the telephone, he was crying. He reached down and picked me up, hugging me tighter than ever. "Pal, first your Mommy left us, now Gary, my boy has left us. It's just you and me, Aunt Cheryl, and Uncle Dennis. Slowly, Pal, we all seem to be leaving. Without saying any more, Dad held me in his lap as he sat in the recliner, crying. It was a long, long silent night.

Next day he tried to explain what happened to Uncle Gary. Dad said Gary was so young, only fifty-two years old. He said Gary was in perfect physical shape. He exercised every day in the employee gym at work. Dad said he even ran in the New York City Marathon. "Pal, that's 26 miles of running. He would not eat anything that had fat in it. Gary was everything that I am not. Why would he die so young?"

Later Dad told me Gary had a brain aneurism while he was at work.

"What is that, Dad?" I said.

As best he could explain, Dad said, "In your body there are all kinds of tube like things that carry the blood where it is supposed to go. Sometimes one of these tubes gets a bubble in the wall of it and it bursts. That, Pal, is an aneurism. That's what happened in Gary's brain; it means almost instant death."

"Is that," I said, trying to understand, "like when you

were pulling me around last year in my bicycle tow cart and your bike tire suddenly went flat. You came home and took the tube out of the tire. You said the tube was weak in one spot, and the bubble on the tube broke, and the tire went flat. Is that what happened with Uncle Gary's blood tubes, Dad?"

"Pal, I couldn't have said it better."

"Dad," I questioned, "Where did Gary go?"

"Pal, Gary went to Heaven. Now he is in Heaven with his Mommy. Someday, Pal, I'll go to be with them too."

"I hope not, Dad; nobody would be here to take care of me."

"Sure, Pal, there would be Aunt Cheryl to take care of you if I had to leave like that."

"*Dad?*"

"Yes, Pal."

"Do pets go to Heaven too?"

"I'd like to think so, Pal."

"How about those mean old stray cats and the stinky skunk that was in the backyard, and the snake that was in the house the last time Uncle Timmy and Uncle Matthew stayed here all night.

Dad was in an understanding mood and answered, "Yes, Pal, I'm sure God has a place for …" Dad paused. "Did you say a snake in the house?"

"Sure, Dad, it was a wiggly brown and orange thing."

Dad, thinking it was a joke of the worst kind, questioned me, saying, "What did the boys do? Did they catch it?"

"They discovered it behind Mom's big bedroom door when they went to bed. Uncle Matthew went to the kitchen and got the big trash can. Uncle Timmy chased it into a trash bag that was inside the trash can. Then Uncle Timmy tied a knot in the bag so it couldn't get out."

"So, Pal, what did they do with it?

"Uncle Timmy took it down the street and let it loose. He said the snake's mommy was probably looking for him, just like Cheryl looked for me when I got lost. Remember?"

"Uh-huh." was all Dad could say.

Aunt Terri came to stay with me again while Dad, Aunt Cheryl, and her boys went to Pennsylvania for Uncle Gary's funeral. It was sad when Dad left, but Aunt Terri entertained me a bunch and took good care of me. We went across the street and visited with Aunt Jamie and Uncle Tom a lot. For me life was good, for Dad, not so good.

A couple of weeks after Dad came home, we went to Aunt Cheryl's house again. Aunt Cheryl had some work for Dad to do in her backyard. While Dad was outside working in the backyard, some of Uncle Timmy's friends came by for a visit. Aunt Cheryl has a swimming pool at her house and the boys tried to get me to go in the water. I really didn't want to do it. I ran around the pool, but they caught me and threw me in the pool. I often wondered if I could swim. Now I know I can, but I still I don't like it. Aunt Cheryl came out and rescued me. "No more swimming pool for Pal!" she told the boys. While she was scolding the boys, I ran to the backyard with Dad and played in the pile of dirt Dad was making. He wasn't particularly happy about that, but I sure was. Kids like to play in the dirt; and remember, I'm still just a little kid, you know.

I like it when Uncle Timmy comes to our place to stay

overnight. If Aunt Cheryl stays overnight at our house, Dad puts the air mattress on the living room floor for Timmy to sleep on. Uncle Timmy is a good sleep buddy; he doesn't toss and turn like Dad does, and he never chases me off his pillow like Aunt Terri. Uncle Timmy is a real friend. I like him a lot!

Having Timmy sleep at our house is fun, but I still like to sleep with Dad. Not long ago I was sound asleep and apparently I began to dream and cry in my sleep. I felt Dad's hand reach over and gently stroke my back, as he said, "You must have been dreaming, Pal; close your eyes and go back to sleep. I'm still here with you. Okay?"

There was another time I was laying sideways in the bed, but tight against Dad's body. Apparently I began dreaming again. "Yes, folks, dogs dream too!" Anyhow I have no idea what I was dreaming about, but I began kicking Dad in the stomach with my hind legs. This time he placed his hands under me and turned me away from him. Now he knows how it feels when he kicks me during his tossing and turning at night.

CHAPTER 17

. . . .

Dad's Old and I'm Catching Up

There's not a whole lot going on around the house these days. As we dogs get older we learn to behave and not cause so much trouble. I guess your personality changes as you get older.

Dad sits at his computer and does a lot of writing stuff. I have no idea what he writes about, but he sure does a lot of it. Someday maybe he will tell me what he is writing.

Dad and I were talking one day about age. Dad said, "One day, Pal, you will be as old as me."

"I don't think so, Dad!"

"Sure you will, Pal! You were just 5 years old. Right? Now, in people years that makes you at least 35. One year in dog years equals about 7 years in people years."

"That's silly, Dad! I'm a dog, not a people!"

"You act and talk like a person, don't you?"

I couldn't argue with him about some of that. "But, Dad, I have papers that say I'm a dog."

"I know you are, but think about it. Using the people formula for age, when you are 10½ you will be a little over 73. I had a birthday last year and I was 75. So you see, Pal, you will be older than me some day."

The conversation ended with me scratching my head and saying, "Hmm … very interesting this people age thing!"

Mark Twain once said, "There is no such thing as an uninteresting person." This story apparently proves those words to be true. Pal is definitely an interesting person … even if he *is really a dog!*

ABOUT THE AUTHOR

. . . .

Lee A. Drayer

My life began during the late depression years in October 1934. Our home was located in a small Pennsylvania town, New Cumberland, located across the river from the capital city of Harrisburg.

As a child, day dreaming was a serious problem for me. Lack of attention throughout grade school and high school presented a very real challenge for my school teachers and my dad.

My mother died suddenly and left my dad a very frustrated parent as he attempted to deal with the unruly boy I had become. The result, I was sent to a private orphan school in Hershey, Pennsylvania.

It was there I met my first and last love. We spent almost fifty-four years together before she died. Three great children later, here I am at age seventy-six, still daydreaming, but using my creative imagination to write books.

What you have read is what Pal told me to write. That's my excuse and I'm sticking to it!

In 1975 my wife and I moved to Florida. Presently live in the Four Corners area near Davenport, Florida, alone but with my dog, Pal.

Until recently I had never read a book in school or any other time. While visiting my oldest son's home in 2007, I found two books on his bookshelf and read them to help pass the time. It was then I realized, reading really is fun. Shortly thereafter I decided; why not try writing a book. This book is one of the results.

Working part-time now allows me the opportunity to do what I really enjoy; writing books. My first book, *I Am That I Am,* also published by **Trafford Publishing**, became available in September, 2009. Reading and writing books has become a pleasurable way to enjoy my retirement years.